# GREAT AUNT ESME'S PASTY SHOP

Daphne Neville

ISBN: 9798784513496

PublishNation
www.publishnation.co.uk

# Other Titles by This Author

TRENGILLION CORNISH MYSTERY SERIES
*The Ringing Bells Inn*
*Polquillick*
*Sea, Sun, Cads and Scallywags*
*Grave Allegations*
*The Old Vicarage*
*A Celestial Affair*
*Trengillion's Jubilee Jamboree*

PENTRILLICK CORNISH MYSTERY SERIES
*The Chocolate Box Holiday*
*A Pasty in a Pear Tree*
*The Suitcase in the Attic*
*Tea and Broken Biscuits*
*The Old Bakehouse*
*Death by Hanging Basket*
*Murder in Hawthorn Road*

*The Old Coaching Inn*
*The Old Tile House*

# Chapter One

The sun disappeared behind a threatening grey cloud as Lottie Burton unpegged sheets, duvet covers and pillow cases from the washing line in the back garden of Primrose Cottage. Glad the morning had stayed fine long enough to dry the bedlinen, she returned to the kitchen, hung the folded items on a clothes horse to air and placed it by the dining room window hoping the sun would show its face again. As she returned the box of pegs to the cupboard beneath the sink, she heard her twin sister's car pull up on the tarmacked area beside the garage. Lottie reached for the kettle as the car door slammed shut. "Tea, Het?" she called as the front door opened, "or would you prefer coffee?"

Hetty entered the kitchen with two large bags of groceries and placed them on the table: "Tea please, Lottie." Before she took off her jacket she pulled a homemade cotton mask from her pocket and tossed it into the empty washing machine.

Lottie aware of her sibling's glum face opened a packet of chocolate digestive biscuits while she waited for the kettle to boil hoping a sweet treat might cheer her sister up.

"Is the washing in yet? It's raining in Penzance." Hetty glanced outside as she placed a new bottle of washing-up liquid on the window sill. Seeing the line was empty she knew the answer. "No, need to reply. I can see you did." Hetty folded up the empty shopping bags and placed them in the cupboard, "Not only was in wet in Penzance, Lottie,

1

but it felt chilly too. More like October than August. Still, perhaps we'll have an Indian summer."

"Maybe, but there's still a couple of weeks left in this month so things might improve before then."

Hetty grunted and sat down heavily on one of the kitchen chairs.

"What's the matter, Het?" Lottie placed two mugs on the table, "You look proper fed up."

"Oh, I don't know. Just everything, I suppose. Fatigue, the unknown and another winter looming ahead."

Lottie sat down opposite her sister. "Oh dear, it's not like you to let things get you down."

"I know and I try to stay positive but it's been such a funny eighteen months with the Covid thing, hasn't it? No bingo this summer or last year, no gardening club or drama group meetings. No Pentrillick in Bloom competition either. Zac and Emma have had to put off their wedding umpteen times and we still don't know when it'll be."

"They're young, they've plenty of time," Lottie reached out and gently patted her sister's hand. "As for the pandemic, well, we're still here, Het and so are the family and our friends. Lots haven't been so fortunate. Instead of wallowing in self-pity you really should count your blessings. I do every day."

"I know, I know and you're right, as usual, so take no notice of me, I'm just being grumpy." As she spoke they heard the sound of a heavy vehicle stop outside in the lane.

Lottie looked at the kitchen clock. "That'll be Ginny and Alex's removal van. They said it was due here around midday."

Hetty groaned. "And that's another thing making me feel low. Ginny and Alex going. Goodness knows what the new neighbours will be like and never having met them, Ginny can't tell us anything about them. She couldn't even remember their names when we saw her the other day." Hetty dipped her biscuit in her tea so the chocolate melted, "Oh, and she knows they're moving from somewhere in the London area, not that that's much help."

"Well, I suppose she has a lot on her mind and the names of the new people don't really matter to her and Alex as they'll never meet them," Lottie's face broke into a broad smile, "Anyway, look on the bright side, Het. Having new neighbours means we'll have something to occupy our time during the long winter months. Finding out what we can about them, I mean. You'll like that and so shall I."

"Yes, you're right but whatever they're like, they'll never be as nice as Ginny and Alex. I'll really miss them. They've been good friends as well as perfect neighbours."

"They have, but there's no reason why the new people won't be just as nice. What's more, Het, we've yet to find out what's going to happen to the antiques shop. Workmen have been there for a week or more now and you never know, it might open up as something really interesting."

Ginny and Alex Copeland were already living at Hillside, the house next door to Primrose Cottage, when the sisters moved to the village in December 2016. As well as running and owning the antiques shop on the main street in Pentrillick, Alex was also a driving instructor. The reason for their move away from Cornwall was for them to be nearer Ginny's aged parents in Scarborough; meaning they had not only to sell their home but their antiques shop too. However, realising not many people might be interested in antiques, they sold off most of their stock at half price or less and anything left was donated to the village's charity shop. The premises were then put on the housing market as a viable shop or with the necessary planning permission the opportunity to turn it back into a domestic residence. For the building, originally a semi-detached house, had a large ground floor area; four bedrooms on the first floor and a good sized space in the attic which would easily make two more rooms. However, the upper rooms, which had not been lived in for many years, were in dire need of refurbishment; something Ginny and Alex had always planned to do but never seemed to get round to. Hence there was a little excitement in the village as to what the premises might become. For although shops in general had suffered over the years with on-line shopping, those in Pentrillick thrived especially during the summer months in the holiday season. Meanwhile, another popular business was in the throes of changing hands; after twenty years the owners of the fish and chip shop were retiring at the end of August and moving away to a cottage in South Devon.

Three hours after the removal van had arrived at Hillside there was a knock on the front door of Primrose Cottage. Hetty answered to find their neighbours standing outside in the drizzling rain. Ginny held a large bunch of flowers and Alex a bottle of wine and a box of chocolates. After an emotional farewell, they all promised to keep in touch. The sisters then watched their neighbours drive away for the last time, closely followed by the removal van. As the vehicles disappeared round the corner, the heavens opened and torrential rain fell from the dark, grey clouds.

Later that same day a second removal van pulled up in Blackberry Way and parked by the gates of Alex and Ginny's former home. On hearing its engine stop, Hetty and Lottie ran upstairs to get a better view and were just in time to see two removal men jump down from their vehicle. To the surprise of the sisters, the removal men were greeted by a tall, dark haired man, who emerged from the house. A silver BMW stood in the driveway.

"Well, blow me. I didn't hear that car arrive. Did you, Lottie?"

"No, I didn't. We slipped up there, Het."

"We did, but at least we've had the chance to see one of our new neighbours and I'm pleased to say he looks quite presentable. I just hope the rest of them are too."

"Will there be any more though, Het? I mean, it could be just him."

"No, there has to be a female because Ginny said there were two people named on all the legal stuff."

"Ah yes, she did, and if my memory serves me right she said even though she couldn't remember them, the surnames were different so it looks like they're not married. Whoever they are."

The sisters watched as the removal men carried a cream coloured leather sofa into the house.

"Fancy a cup of tea, Lottie? I mean, we could be up here for some time."

"Yes, please and I must put something warmer on as it feels quite chilly now the rain has stopped."

"Right you are, back in a mo."

While her sister was downstairs, Lottie put on a thicker cardigan and then took spare pillows from her wardrobe and placed them on the window seat for added comfort. She then continued her surveillance, thankful that visibility was clear and the sun was attempting to shine through the thinning clouds.

"I've seen her," squeaked Lottie as Hetty placed two mugs of tea on the window ledge, "and she looks really nice too. She's tall. Well taller than you and me anyway. Her hair is light brown and short and she's slim."

"Age?" Hetty sat down on one of the pillows.

"In her forties, I should imagine. The same as her bloke."

"Excellent, and you know what, Lottie. I've a sneaky feeling that the coming weeks and months won't be too bad after all."

5

# Chapter Two

On Monday morning, three days after the new people had moved into Hillside, Lottie, having noticed the curtains in the sitting room were looking grubby, was standing on a dining chair taking them down when she saw the next door neighbour's BMW pull out into the lane driven by the male member of the household. While pondering where he might be going, the female member left the house and walked along Blackberry Way towards the turning into Long Lane and the village.

"I suppose he'd be going to work," reasoned Hetty, washing dishes in the kitchen as Lottie relayed the news, "I mean, if he's in his forties he'll be a long way off retirement."

"That's just what I thought and she's probably popping down to the shops."

Hetty dried her hands and reached for the tea towel. "Do you think we ought to nip round and welcome them to Pentrillick? Not now of course because they're not there. But later maybe. After all they've been here for three days now and we've not met them yet."

Lottie placed the curtains in the washing machine ready to wash the following day when the weather was forecast to be dry. "I don't know. I mean, do people still do things like that?"

"Probably not but I feel we're being unneighbourly if we don't and I really would like to know something about them. At the moment we don't even know their names."

"We don't so I suggest we give it some thought and see if we can come up with a reason to visit them without us looking nosy."

However, a reason to visit was not necessary for later that morning during a shower of rain, their friend Kitty Thomas who lived at the far end of Blackberry Way, called in for a chat.

"Guess what?" Kitty said as she shook her umbrella and placed it on the doorstep.

"You've met our new neighbours." Hetty was hopeful.

"How did you know?"

"Wishful thinking," called Lottie from the sitting room.

Hetty sat down in her favourite chair and Kitty joined Lottie on the sofa. "So what can you tell us, Kitty?" Hetty tapped her fingernails on her teeth in anticipation.

Lottie tutted. "Should we not offer our guest coffee first, Het?"

"Usually, yes, but on this occasion, no. Coffee can wait. News of our new neighbours is far more important."

Kitty smiled. She understood Hetty's way of thinking. "Well, their names are David and Margot. I assume they're not married because her surname is Osborne and his is Bray. I've just walked up from the shop with Margot so she could shelter under my brolly. She was in there, you see, putting in a regular order for some magazine or other and when she gave her address I realised who she was and so introduced myself as a near neighbour. She seemed really pleased I'd spoken to her and was very friendly. Next week she starts work as café manageress at the supermarket where your son Bill works, Lottie. She's been transferred apparently from wherever she was before."

"Oh, that's lovely. I must give Bill a ring and make sure he gives her a nice warm welcome."

Hetty agreed. "Yes, and once they've become acquainted we'll have a link and a reason to invite Margot and whatever her bloke's called round for a coffee."

"David," Kitty reminded her, "he's David Bray."

"Thanks, Kitty. I must remember that."

"So where were they living before?" Lottie asked.

"London somewhere, wasn't it?" said Hetty. "I'm sure that was one of the few thing Ginny was able to tell us about them."

"That's right," acknowledged Kitty, "but I'm not sure exactly whereabouts in London they were; I do know David was an officer with the Met though and he's been transferred down here because it's where he was born and bred. Not Pentrillick, I might add, but somewhere in Cornwall."

Hetty gasped. "He's a police officer."

Kitty chuckled. "He is, and not just any old police officer. He's a detective inspector."

"What! We're going to have to be on our best behaviour from now on then. No more poking our noses into strange goings on and so forth." Hetty felt quite saddened by the prospect.

"So do they have any pets? Dogs, cats or whatever?" Lottie's incongruous question was prompted by Hetty's dog Albert stretching in his basket.

"Not as far as I know. Margot didn't have a dog with her this morning anyway. They do have a son though. At least Margot does. He's not David's, you see."

"A son," repeated Hetty, "We've not seen hide nor hair of him, so what's he like?"

"A teenager. He's called Derek but he hates his name and insists everyone calls him Dee."

"So is he going to attend school in Penzance?" Lottie asked.

"No, he's eighteen so has left after having done abysmally in his A-Levels."

8

"Which of course he didn't take because of the Coronavirus, poor lad." Lottie having two granddaughters aged nineteen could sympathise because they had been unable to sit their A-Levels the year before.

Kitty laughed. "I don't know about that. According to Margot his grades would probably have been even worse had he sat the exams. His heart wasn't in it, you see. He wants to be a musician and only went on to do further education to appease his mum. He's actually a bright lad and did really well in his GCSEs but went off the boil after that and of course Covid didn't help."

"Dear oh dear. Such a shame but you can't put old heads on young shoulders." Lottie thought again of her two granddaughters: twins, both diligent workers and very ambitious. Kate was interested in law and Vicki in medicine.

"Are the girls looking forward to going back to university?" Kitty asked as though reading Lottie's mind.

"Oh yes. They're enjoying being at home and working in the pub again but I get the impression they miss their new friends and won't be sorry to go back. They've still another month at home yet though, but then you know how time flies."

"Doesn't it just." Kitty pulled a tissue from her pocket and with it came the card of a letting agency. "Oh, before I forget, we have new tenants moving into Fuchsia Cottage tomorrow."

"Goodness gracious me. With all the comings and goings, Blackberry Way is currently a hive of activity," chuckled Lottie.

"That's just what Tommy said."

"So, come on, Kitty. Who and what are the new tenants?" Hetty asked.

"Window cleaners. Apparently they've been running their own business somewhere up-country and decided to move down here and start afresh, meaning

9

they'll have to drum up new customers and so forth. Tom said they're brothers, their surname's Sharpe and with them will be their girlfriends. I don't really know much more than that but they sound reliable and have paid three months' rent in advance."

"You've not met them then?" Hetty stood up.

"No, it was all done on the phone with the agents, but when Tommy heard their trade he said that was good enough for him."

"So what do the girlfriends do?" Lottie asked.

"I've no idea."

Hetty walked towards the door. "Anyway, I think you've earned that cup of coffee, Kitty, so I'll put the kettle on now and then we can chew over what you've told us."

Kitty Thomas and her husband, Tommy, had been together for a little over four years. Near neighbours in Blackberry Way, the retired pair were married following the death of Tommy's widowed mother and made a home together at Meadowsweet, Kitty's house at the far end of the lane leaving Tommy and his late mother's home, Fuchsia Cottage, empty. After much deliberation they decided to rent out the cottage rather than sell it as the extra income would help boost their state pensions. Before they were married, when Tommy looked after his aged mother, he did a spot of window cleaning to keep body and soul together and enjoyed the work, hence his approval of the Sharpe brothers, in line with their girlfriends, to rent his former home.

An hour later when Kitty left, Hetty closed the front door and caught sight of her reflection in the hall mirror. Tutting loudly she picked up the phone. "I am going to ring the hairdressers, Lottie. My hair's a mess and it's driving me mad."

"But I thought you said you'd not get it cut until you were allowed in without a mask."

10

"I did say that but it's just occurred to me that a mask might be a good thing. You see, I hate looking at myself in the mirror while they're doing my hair. The light is so intense I'm sure it picks out wrinkles and grossly exaggerates them. But if most of my face is covered up I can pretend the wrinkles aren't there. As they say, every cloud has a silver lining."

Lottie took a pair of curtains from a chest in the hallway to hang in the sitting room as a temporary measure. "Were I a chap I'd say that was female logic."

"There's nothing wrong with female logic, Lottie. Nothing at all."

# Chapter Three

Two days later, Hetty left Primrose Cottage beneath her umbrella and walked to the end of Blackberry Way into Long Lane and down the hill towards the village. At the bottom she turned left and walked along the main street; her destination, the hairdressers where she had an appointment for a wet cut at ten-thirty.

There were very few people around for the rain was heavy. Hetty cursed as the strong wind buffeted the umbrella she held tightly with both hands afraid it might turn inside out. Before she reached the church she gave up the fight, took down the umbrella and pulled up the collar of her raincoat. For she reasoned that as she was going to have her hair washed anyway the fact it would be wet to begin with was of no consequence.

After passing the church she continued along the road and around the bend chuntering about the weather until she saw a builders' lorry parked on the side of the road outside the former antiques shop. Intrigued as to its new purpose she slowed her pace and on reaching the shop looked at the window. To her disgust it was still whitewashed over and the interior could not be seen. The shop door, however, was wide open and as she peered inside a stocky, middle-aged man pushed out a wheelbarrow full of rubble, thrust it up a plank of wood and tipped it into the back of the lorry. Hetty smiled sweetly. "Good morning, lovely day," she said brightly without thinking.

The man adjusted his wet cap, glanced up at the dark sky and then cast her a pitying look. "I've known better, love."

Hetty cursed beneath her breath. She had been so focused on asking the shop's future she'd not thought out her strategy properly. Feeling foolish she walked briskly on.

Inside the hairdressers, Karen Walker was ready and waiting for her client and once her hair was washed, Hetty sat down in front of the mirror and watched as Karen trimmed her dyed brown curls. After briefly discussing the weather, the number of tourists in the area and other topical news, Hetty asked the question burning her lips. "Any idea what's going on in the old antiques shop, Karen? When I walked by just now I saw a chap tipping rubble onto the back of a lorry, so whatever they're doing looks quite drastic."

"Yes, I do know. According to Nicki it's going to be a pasty shop. Isn't that right, Nicki?"

Standing behind a chair across the room, Nicki Timmins removed curlers from Sally Oliver's dark grey hair. "Yes, that's right. My boyfriend works for the builders who have the job. They're working flat-out and say the owners hope to have the shop up and running by early September at the latest. Apparently the shop part's done and the decorators are due to start in a couple of days but there's more to do out the back still where they've knocked two rooms into one to make a bigger kitchen. The rubble you saw is most likely from the wall they took down because they dumped it out the back as a temporary measure. I know that because I was invited in for a nose round the other day."

"You were? I envy you that," chuckled Hetty, "We've been wanting to know what's going on for a while now. A pasty shop though! I'd never have guessed that in a month of Sundays. So will they sell other stuff as well?"

Nicki shrugged her shoulders. "Not sure, but they're having an area where people will be able to eat their pasties so I suppose they might sell other things too. You know, drinks, chips and so forth."

"And the pasty business is quite diverse now anyway," said Karen, "You know, big, medium, small, cocktail, meat, cheese, veggie, vegan…"

"…Ow, don't, you're making me feel hungry." Hetty's breakfast had consisted of one grapefruit.

"Me too," laughed Sally, "I reckon once I start on pasties I'll need to take up running as well as swimming."

Hetty, aware that Sally was a similar age to herself, looked on admiringly. "Do you still go for a dip every other morning, Sal?"

"I do unless the sea's too rough. I must admit when it is I'm sometimes tempted but Robert always tells me not to be so daft. That's the beauty of living where we do. I can see what the conditions are like without stepping outside."

Sally Oliver and her husband, Robert, both keen gardeners, were in their late sixties and had moved from Birmingham to Pentrillick early in 2019. They lived in a flat over the village's charity shop where they were able to enjoy uninterrupted views of the sea. Although retired, both had secured jobs at Pentrillick House. Robert worked part-time in the gardens and Sally worked on the bowling green.

Much to Hetty's delight the rain had eased when she left the hairdressers but the wind was as strong as ever. To protect her hair she pulled a scarf from her handbag and tied it securely over her head. She then crossed the road in order to avoid the builder she had encountered outside the old antiques shop. As she passed Sea View Cottage, she observed two cars parked in the gap by its side which had not been there earlier. The house belonged to playwright Brett Baker, and people with whom he was acquainted often stayed there as did Brett himself occasionally. Not recognising either car as Brett's she continued along the street and called in at the shop for a bottle of wine and a jumbo bag of her favourite crisps to celebrate discovering the future of the erstwhile antiques shop. Further along the road the fish and chip shop displayed a notice saying the shop was to be closed over the Bank Holiday weekend and would be re-opening on Tuesday August 31$^{st}$ under new ownership. Hetty chuckled to herself. "It's all happening in Pentrillick."

The following morning a car pulled up on the driveway of Primrose Cottage and from it stepped, Debbie, a friend of the sisters.

"Guess what," gasped Debbie, as Hetty opened the door.

"That's just what Kitty said the other day." Lottie stood in the hallway with the vacuum cleaner having just hoovered the stairs.

"Oh, so you already know." Debbie seemed disappointed.

"Well, if it's about the new bloke next door being a copper, yes we do." Hetty closed the front door and indicated Debbie go into the sitting room.

"Is he? I didn't know that. It's good though, isn't it? Because if there's any dodgy stuff going on in the village we'll be able to wheedle information out of him."

"I doubt it," laughed Hetty, "He's a tall bloke with a serious face and looks far from manipulable."

"That's a shame. So what's he called?" Debbie sat down on the sofa.

"Derek," said Hetty, "We've not met him yet but Kitty told us his name."

Lottie tutted. "No, Het, he's called David. Derek is the wannabe musician son who likes to be called Dee and flunked his A-levels."

"I'll put the kettle on," said Hetty.

"Hetty's had her hair cut," said Debbie, as Hetty left the room. "I thought she wasn't going to until she could go without wearing a mask."

"She capitulated and she's quite glad she did because she found out what's going to happen to the antiques shop."

"She did?"

"Yes, it's going to be a pasty shop."

"A pasty shop! Oh, that's a shame. I was hoping it'd be a clothes shop or better still, a shoe shop. Still, never mind. So tell me what you know about your new neighbours."

Lottie sat down beside Debbie and told her all they had gleaned so far. As she finished, Hetty walked in with a tray holding three mugs of coffee and slices of fruit cake.

"It occurred to me while I was in the kitchen that if you didn't know about our neighbours then what's the reason for your visit? Not that it isn't always nice to see you." Hetty put down the tray: "I'm thinking of your 'Guess what' statement."

"Oh yes, of course, silly me. It's about the people staying at Sea View Cottage. You'll never guess who they are."

"Well, considering they could be not only anyone in this country but anyone in the world, providing they abide by travel restrictions of course, that's not an easy thing to guess." Hetty sat down, picked up a slice of cake and broke it in two.

"You're right, Het, so I'll tell you. There are four of them and they're none other than the Hamiltons."

"Hamiltons?" Hetty was confused.

"I didn't explain that very well, did I? What I should have done is emphasised the 'the', because they are *the* Hamiltons?"

Lottie gasped. "As in the thespian lot?"

16

"Yes, Bentley, Angie, Serena and Drake. Britain's famous theatrical family, stars of the West End."

"Are you sure, Debbie?" Hetty was almost speechless.

"Yes, hubby and I went to the Crown and Anchor last night for a meal. No particular reason I might add other than we want to support them all we can after the rotten eighteen months they've had. Anyway, Tess was working and she told us. And it's definitely true because she's Sea View's housekeeper so is always in the know as to who's staying there."

"Well, I never," smiled Hetty, "that'll get the old tongues wagging."

"So why are they here?" Lottie asked, "I mean, I thought the theatres were all back to normal now."

"They are but a couple of days ago there was a fire in the theatre their show's in and so the show's curtailed until repair work is done or they can secure another venue. Sad really, I almost feel sorry for them after their long period with no work."

"Really! I've not heard it mentioned on the news," said Lottie.

"I vaguely remember seeing something on the internet about a fire at a theatre somewhere but read no more than the headlines," Hetty confessed.

"So, how long are they here for?" Lottie having finished her coffee picked up a slice of cake.

"At least a month so I've heard. Unless they find another theatre but even if they do it'll take a while to get the props and stuff moved and in situ, and according to Tess some of it will need to be replaced because it was damaged in the fire."

"Well the West End's loss is our gain," said Lottie, "and their presence might add a little glamour and excitement as we approach the darkening days of autumn."

"Don't say that," scolded Hetty, "about darkening days, I mean. It's not even September yet."

When Debbie rose to leave, Hetty and Lottie went outside with her to wave as she left. In the garden of Hillside next door a young man was sitting on the front doorstep strumming a guitar in the dappled shade of a cherry tree. Hetty tutted. "Look at his untidy hair and tatty clothes. He looks a right oik."

"Shush, Het, he'll hear you." Lottie was shocked by her sister's outspokenness.

"No he won't. He's in a world of his own and I doubt he's even seen us."

Debbie opened the door of her car. "Well he might look a bit of a ragbag but he has a nice face."

"And he can play a nice tune on the guitar as well," said Lottie.

Hetty realising she was outnumbered refrained from making further derisive comments.


Later in the day, as Lottie was putting out the recycling for collection the following morning, she saw their new neighbour, Margot, planting bulbs in a tub by the front door of Hillside. Keen to make her acquaintance, Lottie leaned over the hedge and introduced herself. Margot, having heard a little of the sisters through Kitty, asked Lottie to join her for a cup of tea and to bring her sister along also.

The sitting room of Hillside was unrecognisable. For although the walls were still painted in duck egg blue and the carpets were the same, everything else was different. The curtains were bright and cheerful, there were minimal ornaments on display and the furniture was modern. A complete contrast to the dark antiques favoured by Ginny and Alex.

The sisters learned from Margot that her partner David was currently at work and her son Dee was in his room supposedly practising his guitar. She said how much David liked his new colleagues and was thrilled to be back in Cornwall. They also learned both she and David were keen gardeners and that Margot might well be tempted to join the village's drama group. All in all the meeting was a success and the sisters slept well that night knowing the new inhabitants of Hillside might turn out to be every bit as nice as their erstwhile neighbours, Ginny and Alex.

# Chapter Four

The weather greatly improved during the last week in August and the forecast for the Bank Holiday weekend predicted it would be dry, sunny and warm. Consequently, by day the beach at Pentrillick was busy with holiday makers and locals alike and the Crown and Anchor's clientele spilled onto the pub field. While in the evenings, the unmistakable smell of barbecues wafted across the village in the light south-easterly breeze.

On the Sunday morning of the Bank Holiday weekend, Hetty and Lottie slowly ambled down Long Lane on their way to church. Both wore summer dresses, sandals and straw sunhats, and relished the warmth of the sun, a refreshing contrast to the cool, damp days earlier in the month. During the service Hetty even said a little prayer asking that the lovely weather continue throughout September for the benefit of not just herself but the whole nation.

After leaving the church the sisters stood outside in the graveyard sheltering from the heat in the shade of a yew tree, chatting with members of the congregation.

"I see the new pasty shop's opening up on Friday and the fish and chip shop opens under new ownership on Tuesday. So quite an exciting week," said Hetty to Maisie who worked in the village's charity shop. "Any idea who the new fish and chip shop people are?"

"I've not met them but according to Kitty who greeted them when they were moving in yesterday, they're a married couple who she guesses to be in their fifties and their names are Matilda and Garfield Haddock."

"Haddock, you're pulling my leg."

"No, she's not." Kitty, who had played the organ during the service, put on her sunglasses as she left the building and walked towards them.

"Well I suppose it'll be easy enough to remember then," chuckled Hetty, "and I'm quite partial to a bit of haddock."

Maisie licked her lips. "Me too, especially smoked in a fish pie."

"Oh yes. Tommy and I like fish pies as well," agreed Kitty."

Talking about food the four ladies finally ambled off towards the lichgate and then out onto the street where Maisie turned left and headed home. Hetty, Lottie and Kitty who all lived in Blackberry Way, went in the opposite direction towards the turning for Long Lane and walked home together.

In the evening, Hetty and Lottie went as usual to the Crown and Anchor for a roast dinner; a routine they started once the pub was allowed to re-open back in May. It was fairly quiet indoors as most of the pub's clientele were sitting outside in the early evening sunshine. Inside, working on the bar were Jackie and Tess; licensees, James and Ella were taking a brief rest before the inevitable busy evening of a Bank Holiday Sunday.

"Any idea who owns the new pasty shop?" Hetty asked, as Tess poured two glasses of wine, "We've heard the new people at the fish and chip shop are Haddocks but are still in the dark as regards the pasty place."

"Well really I should be asking you that seeing as they live up your way."

"They what?" Hetty was flabbergasted.

"They live in Blackberry Way with their boyfriends and are renting Fuchsia Cottage from Tommy and Kitty." Tess placed the glasses of wine on the bar and pushed them beneath the Perspex screen.

"Well, I never," Hetty handed Tess a ten pound note and took a large gulp of wine, "I wonder why Kitty didn't mention it when we saw her this morning."

"Perhaps she doesn't know about the shop. I'm sure she would have said otherwise," Lottie turned to Tess, "We knew about the two chaps and their girlfriends, you see, because Kitty told us when she called in a week or so ago. Apparently the boyfriends are brothers who do window cleaning and they intend to run their own business down here."

"Really, now I didn't know that," confessed Tess, "All I've heard is that the girls stayed in Penzance while the shop work was being done. No doubt as a temporary measure 'til they found somewhere to rent on a long let and I expect their boyfriends were with them."

"I suppose it slipped Kitty's mind to mention it this morning," reasoned Hetty. "After all we were more taken with the Haddocks and the fish and chip shop."

Lottie picked up her glass of wine. "So what can you tell us about the pasty shop, Tess?"

"Not a lot other than it's to be run by the two women. I've not met them but someone said they look to be in their late-thirties/early-forties. Their names are Eve and Dolly and they bought the place with inherited money. Actually, that might be wrong but it's just what whoever told me had heard. Anyway, they're both into catering and what have you so should know their stuff."

"Will they be doing all the baking themselves and serving in the shop?" Lottie asked, "I mean, if they are they'll have very long days."

Tess looked along the bar to make sure no-one was waiting to be served for Jackie had gone outside to collect empty glasses. "I expect they'll be helped by their respective boyfriends for the first few days but I doubt they'll hang around if they're starting up a window cleaning business as they'll need to get some new clients.

Having said that, they probably got a few customers while staying in Penzance."

"Any idea what the lads are called?" Hetty asked.

"Dennis and Jude. Not too sure about the surname but I think it might be Sharpe."

Lottie nodded. "Yes, it is Sharpe because I remember Kitty saying."

"And to date we've seen neither hide nor hair of any of them." Hetty zipped up her bag and hung it over her shoulder.

"You are slipping," chuckled Tess. "Anyway, the girls will have help serving in the shop because a young lad called Eddie who is staying in the caravan on the pub field by himself has secured a temporary job there."

"Really! So who is this Eddie?" Lottie asked.

"Don't really know much about him but he's the friend of a friend of James and Ella's son, Harry. Harry's not here now though, he's gone back to his digs ready for his last year at uni. Anyway, somewhere along the line Eddie heard about the caravan here and rang to see if he could rent it for a while. You've only just missed seeing him as he was in earlier playing pool with your grandson, Zac."

"I thought James and Ella had decided not to open up the field as a campsite until the pandemic is a thing of the past. If it ever is."

"Having someone stay in the pub's one and only caravan who is the friend of a friend of Harry's is hardly opening up the campsite, Het."

"Yes, true, I suppose."

Tess took a sip of water. "I feel sorry for James and Ella after all the money they spent on the pub's extension and the shower block for campers. They've lost two summers now but are hoping that next year things will be back to normal and if so, they'll be advertising the new facilities and we'll be able to welcome our first campers safely."

23

"Good. It'll be nice to see the field in use. Anyway, I'm glad this lad Eddie has made friends with Zac, but why does he want to be down here?" Hetty took another sip of her wine.

"Apparently he's a musician. Played with Rhubarb Chutney, a popular band in Sheffield but of course they were unable to work for ages and eventually decided to split up and do their own things. A couple of days after he got here, James heard on the grapevine that the girls would need help in the pasty shop, so he told Eddie in case he'd be interested. He was and so went along to see them and got the job. That's how we know a bit about the place. Eddie's very outgoing. I met him yesterday and he seems a nice lad. Good looking too."

"Rhubarb Chutney!" chuckled Hetty, "I must admit I rather like that name."

"That's what I said to James. Memorable anyway."

"So how long is he here for?" Lottie asked.

"I don't know but he wants to think things through and enjoy a change of scenery. He also hopes the sea might inspire his song writing ready for when he goes solo."

"Good for him and if he's outgoing he'll be a good advert for the pasty shop."

Lottie nodded. "Very true, Het and so it looks like the poor lad was in a similar situation to the Hamiltons. Being temporarily out of work, I mean."

"Yes, and many others to do with the arts have had a rough time too, but thank goodness things seem to be getting back to some sort of normality," Tess lowered her voice, "Would you believe we have an opera singer staying here."

"An opera singer?" laughed Hetty, "No, I don't believe you."

"Shush," Tess nodded towards a lone man sitting in the corner reading a Sunday newspaper. On the table in front of him sat a half full glass of beer and his mobile phone.

"So what's his name?" Hetty asked, "Not that I'm very familiar with opera singers. In fact I'd struggle to name the three tenor chaps but if I remember correctly they're all Italian."

"Only one is," corrected Lottie. "Plácido Domingo and José Carreras are both Spanish. It was the late Luciano Pavarotti who was Italian."

"Well done, Lottie, I'd never have been able to reel off their names as quick as that."

"My dear Hugh, God rest his soul, had some of their recordings and he listened to them frequently."

Hetty nodded her head in the direction of the pub's guest. "So going back to my question, Tess, do you know the name of the singing chappie over there?"

"His name is Gibson Bailey. I Googled him but it came up with nothing so it's either not his real name or he's not very well known. Anyway, he's staying here for two or three weeks depending how things go. Like most people he says he needs a holiday to chill out before he starts working again."

Hetty chuckled. "Well I never expected to see Pentrillick over run by luvvies and musicians."

"Likewise," agreed Tess, "and I think it's really exciting."

"So have you met any of the Hamiltons yet?" Lottie calculated they'd been in the village for a week and she had yet to meet anyone who had seen them.

"Only Angie. I called with flowers for them with Brett's compliments the day after they arrived and she was the only one there. She was very nice and invited me in for coffee. I liked her."

"Is Angie the mother or daughter?" Hetty asked.

"Mother. The daughter's called Serena. Bentley is dad and Drake's their son."

"That's right," said Hetty, "I remember now. I Googled them you see after Debbie told us they were here, just in case I should ever meet them."

Tess lowered her voice. "Well if you're in here as usual next Sunday you'll see them. They've booked a table in the dining room for half eight because it's Drake's twentieth birthday."

"Really!" Hetty beamed with delight, "Well if there are any left, book us a table for four in the dining room at the same time, please, Tess and we'll give having a roast in the bar a miss next week."

"There are a couple of tables left because we've not told anyone they're coming in otherwise we'd have been inundated with bookings. I know it's safe to tell you two though because you'll not pester them for autographs and stuff like some might." Tess glanced over her shoulder as Jackie returned to the bar with a crate of empty glasses, "I'll jot you down in the diary now before I forget and put your food order in at the same time."

"Lovely," said Hetty.

"Four," said Lottie, as they made their way towards their favourite table, "Have you a couple of dashingly handsome young men lined up to join us?"

Hetty chuckled. "I wish. No, Lottie, the others in our party will be Debbie and Kitty. I know they'll want to be here too."

# Chapter Five

"Welcome, welcome, September the first," sang Hetty at the top of her voice, as she sprang out of bed on Wednesday and opened the windows wide to let in the morning sunshine. "You are one of my favourite months."

"What are you shouting about?" Lottie called from out on the landing.

Hetty opened her bedroom door. "I'm welcoming in the new month."

"I see. Are you ready for breakfast yet?"

"Not quite. I need a shower first but I'll be down in ten minutes so you can start cooking." Hetty danced back inside her room and picked up her clothes.

"Porridge or poached eggs?"

"Poached eggs, please. Oh Lottie I'm so happy and I've a feeling that September is going to be a very memorable month."

Glad to see her sister cheerful and optimistic, Lottie, already washed and dressed, went downstairs to let Albert out into the garden and to start the breakfast.


On Friday morning, excited because the new pasty shop was opening for business and eager to see the shop's interior, Hetty and Lottie, planned on having pasties for their lunch. They were already familiar with the shop's exterior for its name 'Great Aunt Esme's Pasty Shop' had replaced the antiques name board on Wednesday. However, they had been unable to see inside the premises because the window and glass panel in the door were still whitewashed over.

At midday the sisters popped clean face masks into their handbags and set off for the village. They weren't sure whether they'd be required to wear them but carried them just in case the pasty shop was busy. As they walked along the main street a sudden smell of fish and chips wafted across the road. Hetty stopped. "Just a thought, Lottie, but why don't you carry on to the pasty shop and I'll pop over the road and get fish and chips, then we can not only share our purchases but also share information gleaned. I mean the Haddocks are new to the village and so it'd be nice to find out something about them as well."

"Excellent idea, Het. I'll meet you outside the fish and chip shop on my way back."

Lottie hurried along the road; as she passed the village hall she cast a glance at the notice board where a single sheet of paper informed villagers that there would be no events in the hall until the end of September when firstly bingo and then the Saturday morning market would return. Saddened that all events were still not back to normal, Lottie continued along the road. As she neared Great Aunt Esme's Pasty Shop she observed a small queue patiently waiting outside; before she reached it, she pulled her mask from her bag, slipped it on and waited her turn.

Behind the counter two women served customers along with a young man who Lottie assumed to be Eddie, the musician staying in the pub's caravan. All wore a name badge. The taller of two women was called Eve, the other Dolly. After weighing them up, Lottie concluded that whoever had told Tess that the girls looked to be in their late thirties/early forties had made a good guess. Eddie was much younger, probably in his early twenties and even though his face was partly hidden beneath a mask, it was possible to see that he was a good-looking lad. After buying a large cheese and onion pasty, Lottie crossed the

28

road and rushed back along the street. Hetty was already outside the fish and chip shop warming her hands on the package containing her purchase. The sisters then hurried home without speaking so as not to get breathless having agreed it would be better to discuss their encounters with the village's newest arrivals in the comfort of their own home.

"You go first," said Hetty, as they sat down at the table in the sitting room each with a plate brimming with half a cheese and onion pasty, half a battered cod fillet and half a large portion of chips.

"Well, even though I couldn't see his face properly it's obvious young Eddie is a good looking chap and he's very good with the shop's customers too. You know, jovial, lots of banter and so forth. He's clearly much admired by his two female bosses as well."

Hetty shook vinegar over her chips. "Oh dear, that might not go down too well with their boyfriends then."

"No, I shouldn't think they'd be bothered and I doubt either would be Eddie's type anyway. What's more, he's got to be fifteen to twenty years younger than them."

"I see. So what are they like?"

"Chalk and cheese. Eve is tall and slim. I couldn't see much of her hair because she was wearing a cap but it looks like she's a redhead. Dolly on the other hand is about the same height as you and me but a bit on the dumpy side. Her hair's black, probably dyed, long, and was pulled back in a ponytail."

"And what about the shop? Is it nice?"

"Yes, lovely and bright. The walls are a primrose yellow and the woodwork is painted mint green. The shop part is on the left and on the right-hand side is a large empty space which was cordoned off. Dolly served me and so I asked her if it was going to be an eating area. She said yes eventually but they're not planning to open it for a while."

Hetty nodded. "Very wise."

"It's not going to be a full on café though but they are thinking of buying a fryer and selling chips to go with the pasties along with salad and homemade coleslaw, plus tea, coffee and soft drinks. They want to see how it goes and I was pleased to hear her say they don't want to take trade away from Taffeta's Tea Shoppe so they'll not be doing cream teas or anything like that." Lottie dipped a chip in tomato ketchup. "They're not sure whether to do portions of chips to take away either because Dolly said they don't want to take trade from the fish and chip shop as they know better than to upset the locals even though they're aware the shop has just changed hands and so the newcomers are no more local than they are."

"You're right about that," said Hetty, "Matilda and Garfield Haddock are from up North. I wasn't sure where but thought I could detect a hint of Geordie in Matilda's speech, but when I asked, they said they came from Doncaster."

"Well that's probably where they lived before they came here but it doesn't mean Matilda wasn't originally from Tyneside."

"No, I suppose not. Anyway I asked them if they knew young Eddie and his erstwhile band Rhubarb Chutney since he comes from up their way but they said no."

"Probably not their kind of music. Anyway, what are the Haddocks like?"

"Peas in a pod," laughed Hetty.

"Really?" Lottie poured a glass of water from the jug on the table.

"Well yes and no. They're alike in as much as they both have lilac coloured hair wound up in a bun and they both wear glasses. They were also dressed alike in white, smock type coat things and they're of a similar height but Matilda is the heavier of the two and probably by a good few pounds."

Lottie's jaw dropped. "They both have mauve hair and Garfield has a man bun!"

"Yes, and I must admit the colour is very subtle and the man bun suits him because he has a nice face."

"What you could see of it."

Hetty laughed. "Yes but I think from what I've seen I'd recognise him if I saw him maskless."

"Hardly surprising with mauve hair."

Later in the day, Hetty walked along the main street of the village with Albert on his lead. As she neared the pasty shop a young man stepped out onto the pavement bidding farewell to someone as he closed the shop door. Hetty slowed her pace. The young man had to be Rhubarb Chutney Eddie, the musician from Sheffield. She smiled sweetly.

The young man zipped up his jacket and returned the smile. "Hey, I love your dog. What's his name?"

"Albert, named after my late father. And you must be Eddie."

"I am," Eddie stooped down and stroked Albert, "my mum and my step-dad have a little dog and he looks just like this little fellow but he doesn't have a sparkly collar like this. Very posh." He ran his fingers over the diamante studded black leather, "What's more it's given me an idea for what to get Mum next Christmas. She loves her dog and I always struggle to find something different."

"It'd go down well I can assure you. My nieces bought Albert's collar for him last Christmas and people seem to know him now, more by his jewels than his name."

"I'm not surprised." As Eddie stood up he quickly glanced over his shoulder.

"Are you okay?" Hetty wondered why he was frowning.

"What. Oh, yes. No, I'm fine. It's just. Oh I don't know. I expect it's my imagination but I keep getting the feeling I'm being watched. Especially at night as it gets quite dark on the pub field."

"Lonely too, I shouldn't wonder," Hetty looked up and down the street but other than themselves only one other person was visible, "Well, I can't see anyone lurking around at present."

"Me neither so perhaps it is just my imagination."

"Or perhaps you're over-tired. The sea can be very energy-sapping until you get used to it. Anyway, we better get on our way while it's fine. I know there's no rain forecast this evening but there are a lot of grey clouds up there so we better get a move on, just in case, as Albert doesn't like getting wet. It was nice meeting you, Eddie and I hope you enjoy your stay in the village."

"Thank you, and nice to meet you both too." Eddie patted Albert's head and then strode off in the opposite direction to Hetty and her four-legged friend.

# Chapter Six

On Saturday morning, eighteen year old Dee Osborne woke up inside his room at Hillside and looked at the clock on his bedside table. It was five minutes to twelve. He cursed realising he must have gone back to sleep after his mother had called him before she left for work at eight-thirty. He sat up. But what was there to get up for? Another day aimlessly strumming his guitar dreaming of fame and fortune? He needed to get discovered but what were the chances of that happening in a back of beyond place like Pentrillick? He slipped out of bed and stretched his long skinny arms. He didn't disapprove of his mother's partner, in fact he quite liked him. Was proud of him even. I mean, how many of his school friends had been able to boast their potential step-dad was a detective with the Met? He just wished it had stayed that way. His potential step-dad being with the Met. But then if he grew up in Cornwall and liked the place he supposed it was only natural he'd want to come back now he was an old man of forty-nine. Dee picked up the clothes he'd dropped on the floor the previous night and put them on. He'd have a shower later when he'd had something to eat.

Yawning, he ambled downstairs where on the doormat he saw a leaflet. He picked it up, carried it into the kitchen and dropped it onto the table. As he turned to open the fridge the word pasty seemed to jump out at him. He looked at the leaflet closely. It was advertising the newly opened business in the village, Great Aunt Esme's Pasty Shop. As the leaflet fell from his hands onto the floor, he recalled hearing some old biddies talking outside the post office the previous day and one of them saying the bloke working in the pasty shop was a musician staying in a caravan on the pub field and that he was in Cornwall hoping for inspiration as he planned his solo career. In reply another said she'd heard he was a wizard guitarist and had played with a band in Sheffield called Rhubarb Chutney. Without wasting a minute, Dee turned on his heels ran up the stairs at ten times his normal speed, dashed into the bathroom and took a shower. He then put a clean pair of torn jeans and his favourite Iron Maiden T-shirt. After combing his lank, shoulder length, mousy blond hair so that it looked as though it had not been combed, he grabbed his jacket and left the house for the village. A pasty was just the thing to start his day.

On Saturday afternoon, Debbie called at Primrose Cottage. "I've just been chatting with Tess and she's filled me in a bit with the girls in the pasty shop's background and I thought you'd like to hear it."

"You know us too well," chuckled Hetty.

"Have the girls been in the pub then?" Lottie asked.

"Yes, they popped in after work at half five while it was quiet. They didn't have to rush home to get dinner because their blokes were going to meet someone in Penzance who might be able to put some work their way and they were going to grab an Indian takeaway afterwards."

"So what can you tell us, Debbie?"

"Well, they, Dolly and Eve, that is, first met at college back in 1999 where they were doing the same catering course. They got on really well and have been friends ever since. At the time they were both living at home with their respective parents but once they got qualified they rented a place and from there ran an outside catering business.

34

You know, providing food for parties, conferences, weddings, funerals and stuff like that."

"They sound very motivated," said Hetty, "I'm impressed."

"They are and they worked damn hard to build up their business which before long was booming and they were working six days a week and sometimes seven if they had a christening party."

"Wouldn't have much time for socialising then," said Lottie.

"Quite right but they didn't know Jude and Dennis back then. In fact it wasn't until they did the catering for a fortieth birthday party, eighteen years after the girls first met at college, that they were introduced to the Sharpe brothers. Apparently the party was for a friend, and that friend introduced the brothers to them. The four got along really well and went out together when work permitted, that is. Then before long Dolly was paired off with Dennis and Eve with Jude. It was Dennis who on the first anniversary of their meeting suggested they all give up city life and head for the country somewhere. Jude wholeheartedly agreed and after giving it a little thought, Dolly and Eve admitted they liked the idea too."

"Well, I should imagine the pandemic helped them decide as well," said Hetty.

Debbie tutted. "I didn't think of that, but yes, from what we've been fed by the media, lots of people have up-sticked and moved to rural areas. Anyway, as regards finance the brothers said they had a substantial amount of money put by that they'd inherited from their grandfather so between them they should be able to raise a mortgage. Dolly and Eve agreed because they had put aside several thousand pounds over the years too."

"So what made them choose Cornwall?" Lottie asked.

"You could say fate," said Debbie, "Apparently they trawled the internet with an open mind looking for anywhere suitable. Preferably a place where they could live as well as doing their catering. Meanwhile, the lads intended to continue their window cleaning wherever they ended up. When they came across the listing for the antiques shop here they all agreed it sounded good and so came down to see it in May."

"After Covid restrictions were eased a little," said Hetty."

"Yes, so they were lucky there. Anyway, as soon as Dolly stepped inside she had a sudden vision of making and selling pasties in the shop. Eve agreed because if they had a retail business it would mean no more evening work; a notion that appealed to them both. Dennis and Jude, who viewed the place with the girls, agreed the property had huge potential and that in time the upstairs rooms could be renovated to make accommodation for them all. Apparently they went home the same day, made an offer and after it was accepted got the ball rolling. After a while when it looked as though they'd be able to pull the move off they looked for temporary accommodation down here so they could oversee the work and found a caravan in Penzance. Then when everything was under control they looked for something more permanent and found Fuchsia Cottage listed with one of the agents."

"Good old Tess, she never lets us down and of course the shop has helped young Eddie with his finances too," said Hetty.

"It has but I should imagine he has a bit tucked by if the band he was in was as successful as we've been led to believe," said Debbie, "Having said that, I should imagine not being able to play for months on end rather made a hole in it."

Lottie glanced at a leaflet for the pasty shop on the coffee table. "So, whose relation is Great Aunt Esme?"

"Now that I don't know. I asked Tess but she didn't know either."

"Probably made it up," chuckled Hetty.


When Margot arrived home from work she found not only had Dee washed the breakfast dishes as asked, but he also offered to make her a cup of tea. As she sat and removed her shoes she cast him a quizzical glance. "Do I detect a smug look on your face?"

"Maybe," he tried not to smirk.

"And the reason?"

He sat down beside her on the couch. "I went to the new shop today to get myself a pasty and the bloke working there is a musician. He's called Eddie and is a guitarist. He used to play with a band in Sheffield but of course they couldn't do any gigs for ages because of the Covid thing and they've since split up. He's planning to go solo now and while he's here he's gonna write songs and stuff. I told him I'm a musician too and he invited me along to his caravan so we can play together. I'm really excited because I'm sure I'll learn a lot."

Margot rolled her eyes. "It's a bit of an exaggeration to say you're a musician, don't you think?"

"Maybe but if I want to get somewhere I need to mix with blokes like him, Mum."

"Okay. So who is he? Anyone of note?"

"He used to play with a band called Rhubarb Chutney. I've checked them out on social media and they used to have a large following. They released a couple of albums too and I've seen a video of them on YouTube. It's not really my type of music. They come across as squeaky clean the dead opposite to the heavy metal stuff I like, but that doesn't matter because Eddie's brilliant on the guitar and I could learn a lot from him."

"So why is he down here?"

"I've already said, because he's going solo and wants to write songs and stuff."

"Yes, I get that, but why Pentrillick?"

"Oh, I see. It's because he heard through a friend of a friend of the pub licensees' son, who I think is called Harry, that they, the licensees, have a caravan so he rang to ask if he could rent it for a while. The caravan's on the pub field. The landlord said he could stay in the pub if he wanted but Eddie said best not to as his playing might annoy the guests, especially if he's trying new stuff out. And before you ask, he's working in the pasty shop to earn some dosh."

"Sounds good and I hope all goes well. And when you're ready I'll have that cup of tea you offered."

# Chapter Seven

On Sunday evening, Hetty and Lottie prepared for their visit to the Crown and Anchor for a meal with Debbie and Kitty to observe the Hamiltons due in to celebrate Drake's twentieth birthday. Looking forward to an exciting evening, they thoughtfully choose appropriate outfits and applied a little subtle make-up.

It was arranged that Kitty would call for them at seven-thirty and then they would all walk down Long Lane together and meet Debbie in the bar. However, when Kitty arrived she was with her husband, Tommy.

"Don't worry," Tommy said, seeing the surprised look on Lottie's face as she answered the door, "I'm not gate crashing your fancy dinner party hobnobbing with the rich and famous. I'm going down for a pint with Bernie and Sid. And if I get peckish while I'm out, I'll grab a packet of crisps and make myself a jam sandwich when I get home."

Kitty gasped. "Peckish indeed! Don't believe a word of it, Lottie, he's just eaten best part of a shepherds' pie that was more than big enough for two."

"Thank goodness for that, I was beginning to feel guilty." Lottie led them indoors to wait for Hetty who was in the bathroom brushing her hair. As she picked up her jacket, Tommy gave her a friendly nudge, "I hope you don't mind me winding you up."

Lottie nudged him back. "No, of course not. We're sort of used to it. Although you're not as bad as you were when we first met you and you fooled us with a put-on Irish accent."

"Good, and the bit about me meeting Bernie and Sid is true anyway. We've not had a natter for a while and with new folks in the village, celebrities everywhere and a pasty shop too, there's a lot to discuss."


The Crown and Anchor was busier than usual when they arrived and so the ladies had to make do with the least popular table in the bar which Debbie had already secured. As they sat, Tommy bid them farewell and went to join Sid and Bernie over by the piano.

"Sorry about the table," said Debbie, "but it was the only one with no-one on it."

"Not to worry," said Kitty, "we'll be going in the dining room soon anyway."

"Looks like word's got out about the Hamiltons coming in," said Lottie, as she removed her coat and hung it on the back of her chair.

"Hardly surprising." Hetty straightened beer mats on the table that were left skew-wiff, "I mean, can you imagine Tess keeping it a secret for long? Having said that, perhaps James or Ella let it be known, after all it's got to be good for business."

At half past eight, Tess told the ladies their table was ready and so they gathered their belongings together and followed her into the dining room.

"Are the Hamiltons not here yet?" A quick glance from Lottie noted the family were not present.

"No. They rang to say they're running a bit late but should be here by a quarter to nine," Tess nodded towards an empty table, "They'll be going over there so within eavesdropping distance."

"Cheeky," said Hetty, unable to hide her delight.

Tess smiled, she was obviously enjoying the evening. As they sat, she handed them each a menu.

"Are Kate and Vicki waitressing this evening?" Lottie asked.

"No, it's Jade and Juliet tonight. Your granddaughters worked last night," Tess smiled, "They take it in turns but knowing the Hamiltons were in tonight, the twins wanted Jade and Juliet to swap but they both said no chance. It seems all four are madly in love with Drake and Eddie."

Hetty tutted. "Teenage girls today are so fickle. It's usually young Harry they drool over but then I hear he's gone back now."

"They're no more fickle than we were, Het, albeit a long time ago."

After Hetty had decided what to eat, she cast her eyes around the dining room. Over in the corner, tucked in the alcove were the new owners of the fish and chip shop. Garfield held a bottle of wine and was pouring a glass for his wife who was perusing the menu.

"Don't all look at once but the Haddocks are over by the fireplace."

Lottie, Debbie and Kitty simultaneously turned their heads in the indicated direction.

"I'm surprised you recognised them, Het," said Debbie, "I wouldn't have and I've been in twice since they took over."

"What! You must be joking," Hetty laughed, "It's the hair that did it, even though they've abandoned their buns that shade of lilac is quite distinguishable."

"Ah, but I didn't really get a chance to take in their hair colour. Having my back to them only allowed me a quick peek."

"First time I've seen them," admitted Lottie, "and I have to say the pale mauve hair colour suits them as they're both fair skinned."

"You're fair skinned too, Lottie, so will you be dying your hair a pastel shade?" Debbie chuckled at the thought.

"You never know. I might surprise you one day."

"I've not been in the fish and chip shop since they took over," said Kitty, "and even though I had a quick chat with them when they were moving in, I can't for the life of me remember their Christian names."

"Matilda and Garfield," recited Hetty. As she spoke Tess entered the dining room followed by the Hamiltons. The conversation on all tables ceased as the family took their seats around the table beneath a picture of the Crown and Anchor painted by landlady, Ella.

Forty-seven year old Bentley Hamilton was well over six feet tall, had thick, dark brown hair and was immaculately dressed in designer casuals. Angie, his attractive forty-three year old wife with whom he had recently celebrated their silver wedding anniversary, sat opposite him. Dressed in emerald green, her outfit accentuated the colour of her shoulder-length auburn hair. Drake Hamilton whose twentieth birthday they were in to celebrate, wore jeans and a shirt open at the neck. His eighteen year old sister, Serena, sat opposite him and the look on her face indicated that the surroundings were not to her liking. After handing out menus to the family, Tess left the room only to return a few minutes later with a couple who she seated beside one of the three windows on a table for two.

"Well, look who's just walked in," said Kitty, who faced the door, "Your next door neighbours, Debbie."

"Humph," grunted Hetty, "trust her to be here tonight. Obviously tipped off by Tess."

"What, like us you mean?" Lottie was amused by her sister's hypocrisy.

"Okay, fair enough." Hetty watched as the latest arrivals took their seats opposite each other. Gary, a security guard sat facing the window, Marlene, his attractive wife sat facing the room where she had a good view of the Hamiltons' table.

Hetty wanted to comment but thought it unwise and so chose to keep her opinions to herself. For Marlene, a well-liked dinner lady at the village primary school, was a member of the village's dramatic society; she often took the leading role in its productions and even Hetty had to admit that she was talented.

After she and other members of her family had ordered food, Angie Hamilton took a sip of her wine and glanced over the rim of her glass at the other diners. In the corner sat the Haddocks. She caught Matilda's eye and gave her a little wave for she was already acquainted with the fish shop proprietors and liked them immensely. On the other side of the fireplace sat a young couple whom she had never seen before. They kept their voices and heads low and Angie got the impression they had eyes for no-one but each other.

By a window sat a couple who Angie estimated to be of a similar age to herself. Judging by the lack of communication between the two she assumed they were long married and over the years had exhausted every topic of conversation. She could not see the face of the male for his back was to her but the female was all smiles and every time Angie glanced her way she was greeted with a grin of adoration. Angie knew the type well. Always eager to make the acquaintance of celebs just so they had something to tell their friends. Not that Angie considered herself to be a celeb. She hated the expression and thought of herself as just an actress who was doing a job. Feeling sorry for the grinning female, Angie responded with a sweet smile knowing it would have made her day.

At a table in the corner by the door was man alone who she guessed to be the opera singer she had heard was in the village. His back was straight and he looked to be a good height although it was impossible to be sure as he was sitting down. He was a little overweight and his grey hair was thinning but he had a nice face. A kind face and Angie felt sure, were she to get to know him, they would have a lot in common and get on well.

On the next table sat four ladies all of whom she gauged to be in their sixties. The ladies were all nicely dressed; laughed a lot, seemed to be having a good time and Angie half wished she was sitting with them. Not that she didn't want to be with her family. She loved them all deeply despite their shortcomings. Bentley was a dear. Considerate and kind but inclined to be pompous. Drake on the other hand was the complete opposite. Yes, he was kind and considerate but there the similarity ended, for he liked the simple things in life and enjoyed mixing with all people irrespective of their social standing. Serena was like her father but lacked lustre. She thought highly of herself and was inclined to look down her nose at anyone who had not featured in Hello magazine.

When the four ladies finished their meals they returned to the bar.

"Are we having another drink?" Debbie saw that although the bar was busy with drinkers there was one empty table by the French doors.

"Have we time?" Kitty asked.

Hetty looked at her watch. "Yes, it's only a quarter to ten, so three quarters of an hour 'til closing time."

"Good," Lottie sat down and loosened the belt of her skirt, "but I couldn't drink any more wine."

"I think I could manage a liqueur." Hetty cast her eyes towards the bar and the bottles on the top shelf.

Kitty licked her lips. "Hmm, definitely. Baileys and ice for me."

"Oh yes," agreed Lottie, "that'd slip down nicely."

"I'll get them. My treat." Debbie made her way to the bar.

With four glasses of Baileys and ice on their table the ladies chewed over their observations of the Hamiltons and as Lottie was saying how much she liked Angie's dress, the Haddocks emerged from the dining room.

"Evening, ladies," said Garfield, "lovely food they do here."

"Absolutely," said Debbie, "and we're very lucky to have such a fantastic team."

"Come and join us," said Hetty, seeing the Haddocks were looking around for somewhere to sit, "We'd love to chat with you."

"That's if you'd like to," added Lottie.

"We'd be delighted." Matilda indicated to James that they'd like two more glasses of wine and after collecting them joined her husband already seated with the ladies.

"Who's looking after the fish and chip shop tonight?" Kitty asked.

"No-one. I know the previous owners stayed open 'til nine-thirty every night but we've decided to close at seven on Sundays and eight for the rest of the week, except for the summer months when we'll stay open 'til ten. Gotta have a bit of time off," chuckled Garfield.

"I don't blame you" said Lottie, "and once it's dark people don't want to turn out anyway."

"So what brought you down here to Pentrillick?" Hetty asked. "I believe you were in Doncaster before."

"That's right and we're here because we fancied a change," said Garfield. "Originally we thought of buying the old antiques shop and opening it up as a café but when we saw the awful state of the upstairs rooms we decided it'd cost an arm and a leg to get it safe and habitable so ruled it out, as we had to have somewhere to live. It's while we were here looking round we saw the fish and chip shop for sale. It has smashing accommodation upstairs and sea views too so for us it was the perfect place and well, here we are."

"So you'd not run a fish and chip shop before then?" asked Debbie.

"No, but my parents had a café," said Matilda, "and so I grew up sort of knowing the trade. They've retired now of course and their café is now a top notch restaurant run by a celebrity chef. Needless to say it had a very expensive makeover after my folks sold up."

"So what were you doing before you came down here?" Hetty asked.

"We had a music shop," said Garfield, "and it used to do really well before internet sales kicked in."

"Selling musical instruments?" Kitty was a very good pianist who played the church organ on weeks alternating with Debbie's husband, Gideon.

"No," chuckled Garfield, "we sold recorded stuff. You know, records, tapes, CDs and so forth."

"Very nice," said Debbie, "So who are your favourite all time musicians?"

"Guns and Roses," said Garfield without hesitation.

"And we've tickets to see them live in London next June," added Matilda, "As long as this Covid thing permits it, that is. It's already been put back a year."

Hetty frowned. "Who or what are Guns and Roses?"

"Oh, Het," tutted Lottie, "You must remember they were the band Bill liked when he was young back in the eighties and nineties. Always going on about them he was and had all their albums."

"Yes, of course. Silly me."

"Who's Bill?" Matilda asked, "He sounds like my kind of guy."

"My son. He lives in the village in the Old Bakehouse."

"He's a baker," said Garfield.

Lottie laughed. "No, he's a supermarket manager."

"So how long did you have the music shop?" Debbie asked.

"More years than I care to remember," said Garfield, "although to begin with I just worked there. You see, when I was a gangly teenager I fancied myself as a musician but didn't have the talent so I spent a few years being a DJ, feeling that was the next best thing. That meant I was a regular visitor to my favourite music shop and one day while there I saw a notice saying they had a staff vacancy. My dad was always getting on to me about getting a proper job and so I asked about it. Being a regular I knew the proprietors anyway and so they said the job was mine. Mum and Dad were pleased and so everything was perfect. I'd work in the shop five days a week and then on Saturday nights do my regular spot as a DJ. After I'd been there for twenty years the owners retired and so I bought the business from them. Shortly after along came Matilda looking for a part-time job and so I took her on. We were married two years later."

"Oh, that's lovely," said Lottie, "Any children?"

"Not between us," said Matilda, "although I do have a son from a previous marriage. I've not seen much of him over the years though as he preferred to spend time with his dad because they had a lot in common. But he's left his dad's place now and is living in Leeds. He messaged me the other day to ask if we were okay and said if he could get away he'd pop down and see us during the Christmas period."

"So how old is your son?" Debbie asked.

"He'll be twenty two now."

As her words faded, the Hamiltons emerged from the dining room and Bentley thanked James and Ella for their hospitality.

"What do you make of them?" Hetty asked the Haddocks as the Hamiltons made for the door.

"She's alright," said Matilda, "in fact she's brilliant. She pops in most days for a portion of chips on her way back home from a run and we let her eat them out of sight in case Bentley gets to hear. She put on a bit of weight during the lockdowns and says she really ought to lose it hence the running, but she doesn't see the point at the moment as it could be another month or so before their show's up and running again," Matilda took a sip of her wine, "Bless her. She said if she puts on any more weight she'll have to get the wardrobe mistress to let out the seams of her costumes."

"As for Bentley, we've not had reason to speak to him," said Garfield, "but I always get the impression he thinks he's a cut above everyone else, especially down here."

"That's just what we thought," chuckled Hetty, "but being a handsome looking bloke he can get away with it."

# Chapter Eight

Lifelong friends, Maisie and Daisy had lived in Pentrillick since they were born back in the nineteen fifties and for the past seven years had served together as volunteers in the village's charity shop. In their early days they were helped out by Tommy Thomas who worked part-time as a window cleaner. Every other Monday he manned the shop to enable them to have the day off and Cilla Jenkins worked every other Wednesday for the same reason. However, after Tommy Thomas married Kitty he gave up his hours and shortly after that Cilla left the area and moved to Plymouth. Thereafter the ladies ran the shop on their own but cut down the shop's opening hours. It was a job the ladies enjoyed. They loved the fact they were helping sick and unfortunate animals and relished the opportunity to chat with the locals and keep up with village gossip.

On Monday morning, a van pulled up outside the shop and unloaded several boxes of goods, donations from a gift shop that had recently stopped trading. Amongst the items were colourful glass balls, the type once used by fishermen as floats for their nets. Each ball was encased in fine rope latticework. Daisy and Maisie priced the balls and hung them around the shop, but as Maisie went to fold down the cardboard box they had arrived in she noticed a single, clear glass, ball tucked in the corner devoid of rope.

"What shall we do with this?" she held the ball up for Daisy to see.

"Sell it as a crystal ball perhaps?"

"Oh, I like that idea. I'll pop it on the counter."

By the time all the assorted new goods were unpacked it was time to close for lunch. As Maisie locked the door, Daisy glanced at the clear glass ball and chuckled. "Our new crystal ball says we should have a pasty each for lunch."

"What a good idea. I'll go as I'd like to meet the young chap working there who everyone is raving about."

While Daisy tidied up and put on the kettle, Maisie made her way through the village to purchase their lunch at Pentrillick's newly opened business.

Inside Great Aunt Esme's Pasty Shop, Eddie and Eve were serving customers while Dolly was out the back taking a new batch of pasties from the oven.

"You must be the young man I've heard so much about," said Maisie, as Eddie dropped her order of two medium size beef pasties into paper bags, "You used to play with a band up country somewhere, I believe."

"That's right, in Sheffield."

"Oh, that's interesting. Kate, the granddaughter of a friend of mine, goes to uni there. Studying law and criminology. Something like that."

"Oh, I know Kate. She and her sister work in the pub during the holidays. They were there the other night and we got chatting when they finished their waitressing shifts. Big brother, Zac, was in too and trying to get me to join the pub's pool team."

"And did you?"

"I was tempted but it seemed silly as I'll only be here for a few weeks."

Maisie dabbed her debit card on the contactless paying device. "I see, and you're staying in the pub caravan, I believe. Nice spot that and you must be able to hear the sea."

"It is and I can, which reminds me, I keep meaning to ask someone why there's only the one caravan. Looks and feels a bit lonely by itself."

"There used to be more. Can't remember if it was three or four, but James and Ella only had them put on the field for the workmen to stay in when they built the extension and so forth back in 2019, I think it was. The firm came from further up the line, so they stayed here during the week to save driving back home every night."

"I see."

"So, how are you liking the village?"

"I like it a lot. One of your locals came to see me on Saturday night. We both played our guitars and sang. I hope we didn't disturb anyone."

"I've not heard any complaints," chuckled Maisie, "So who came to play with you? I can't think of anyone I know who plays the guitar. Not that I'm familiar with the hobbies of youngsters."

"Chap called Dee. Don't really know any more than that."

"Dee?" Maisie frowned, "Oh, I know, he'll be the lad who recently moved here with his mum and her police officer chap. They live next door to my friends, Hetty and Lottie in Blackberry Way." Maisie picked up the two bags of pasties, "Anyway, nice meeting you, Ed, and I daresay I'll be in again if these are as good as I'm hearing."

"Yeah, cheers. Bye."

"You're getting quite a fan club," laughed Eve, as Maisie left the shop, "I've noticed the ladies always make a bee-line for you and linger with their chat."

"Yeah, maybe and the blokes always make a bee-line for you."

"Oh, do you think so?" Eve was flattered, "I've always considered myself to be a plain Jane."

Eddie raised his eyebrows. "I think you need to look in the mirror more often. You're drop dead gorgeous for a mature woman."

"Mature woman! I'll have you know I'm only thirty-nine."

"Precisely. Just four years younger than my mum."

Eddie ducked as she threw a damp cloth in his direction.

At half past five, Eddie turned the card hanging on the inside of the pasty shop's door from open to closed, dropped the catch and turned the key in a second lock. Because trade trailed off after four o'clock and they had shopping to do, Dolly and Eve left at five o'clock after instructing him to remove the drawer of money from the till and hide it at the back of the cupboard in the hallway where they kept paper bags, ready for either of them to cash up in the morning. As he closed the cupboard door, his mobile phone rang. It was Dee.

"Hi, Ed, fancy another bash tonight?"

"You must have read my mind because I was thinking the same thing only this time with a few beers. I was thinking of asking Drake along too. Be interesting to see what he's up to. Haven't seen him for a nearly a week now."

"Drake, what as in Hamilton?"

"Yeah. You know him?"

"I know of him but I've never met him or seen him for that matter. I know he's staying in the village though."

"That's right, he's down with his folks."

"So how come you know him?"

"My dad and his dad were at school together so we've known each other for years. He's a few years younger than me and also plays the guitar. When he heard some mates and me were starting a band he wanted to join but his dad said no as he was only fifteen at the time. Not quite sure if it was because he wanted him to be an actor like himself and Angie or if he didn't want Drake to go down the music path because it can lead to excessive drinking and drugs." Eddie chuckled, "Not that that applied to us as our image was squeaky clean. Anyway, I'll ring him when I get back to the caravan. I'd do it now but when he gave me his new number my battery was dead so I had to write it down and it's still tucked inside the pocket of my leather jacket. Bit slap-dash of me really. Should have put it on my phone ages ago. Anyway, I'll pop in the shop and grab a few beers on my way home."

"Ideal. So have you finished work now?"

"Yeah, just gotta grab my things, lock up, set the alarm and post the keys through the letterbox. So see you later. Say half sevenish. That'll give me time to have a shower and scribble down words to a song that are going round in my head."

"Yeah, great, I'll be there."

"Good, and don't bother to eat before you come out, then we'll order pizzas later. My treat."


As Eddie stepped onto the pavement and locked the shop door, he saw Kate and Vicki heading his way.

"Hi girls, off to work?" He posted the shop keys through the letterbox.

"Yes," said Vicki, "there are quite a lot of people booked in tonight so we're going in early to help with the prep work."

"Then allow me to escort you. Well, as far as the shop anyway."

"We'd be honoured," laughed Kate, as they fell in step either side of him.

"So what are you up to tonight?" Vicki asked.

"Got Dee coming round again for a music session and probably Drake too but I've yet to ring him."

"Oh, so you won't be in the pub then?" Kate was clearly disappointed.

"Depends what time we wind up. If we finish early we might pop in for a game of pool especially if your brother's there."

"Oh, Zac will be there," said Vicki, "He'll be in every night until the pool season starts. He says he needs the practice."

"Practice! He's red-hot already."

"Not in his eyes he isn't," said Kate.

"Anyway, if you get the chance do pop in," pleaded Vicki, "because we've not met or even seen this Dee bloke yet, even though he lives next door to our gran and great aunt."

"Does he? I didn't know that but then I don't know where he lives and I don't expect I know your gran and great aunt either."

"Oh, I'm sure you'll have seen them out and about," said Kate, "especially Great Auntie Het. She's often out walking her little dog with a sparkly collar…"

"…called Albert after her dad," finished Eddie, "Yes, I've met her. Nice lady. Nice collar."

When they reached the shop Eddie stopped walking. "Well, this is where I leave you, girls. Gotta pop in here to get a few bits for tonight but I'll probably see you later."

"Hope so," Kate linked arms with her sister and they carried on walking towards the Crown and Anchor, thrilled to have seen one of their current idols.


At twenty minutes past seven, Dee left Hillside clutching his guitar case and four cans of lager that he'd scrounged from his mother's partner, David. The light was slowly fading and the sky was an endless blanket of grey as he ambled down Long Lane towards the village where other than the rumbling of the distant sea and the occasional roar of a car's engine along the main street, all was quiet. As he passed an exposed gateway, a sudden gust of wind ruffled his hair. Not wanting to stop, he pushed the cans of lager under the arm carrying his guitar and with his free hand pulled up the hood of his jacket. At that same moment the church clock struck the half hour. Determined not to be a minute later than necessary, Dee hastened his pace, eager to demonstrate to Eddie his enthusiasm to play.

At the foot of the hill he skipped over the road towards the Crown and Anchor and then ran across the car park and onto the pub field where Eddie's silver VW Golf was parked alongside his caravan. The curtains of the caravan were not drawn; beams of light shone from the windows onto the damp grass and Ed Sheeran's voice rang out from a digital radio. Dee climbed the steps and knocked on the door. No reply. He knocked again. Still no reply. Thinking Eddie might have popped into the pub for some reason, he sat down on the top step and rang his number. To his surprise he heard the phone ringing inside the caravan. Assuming Eddie had left his phone behind, Dee decided to wait. Ten minutes passed and still he was alone. As a few drops of light rain fell he stood up and tried the door. It was unlocked; as expected there was no-one inside but eight cans of lager stood on the table top alongside a bottle of vodka, bags of crisps and a mobile phone. Dee decided to wait in the dry. As the church clock struck eight he began to feel uneasy. Not only was Eddie not there but neither was Drake. Dee frowned. Perhaps then Eddie had decided not to invite Drake or that Drake was otherwise engaged and Eddie had for some reason popped into the Crown and Anchor and lost track of time. There was only one way to find out. He stood up and left the caravan to see if his surmise was correct.

It was the first time Dee had set foot in the pub for being new to the area and having no friends to go out with it wasn't somewhere he'd been enticed to visit. On entering the public bar he looked around hoping to see a familiar face but to his dismay saw no-one he knew. James the landlord was behind the counter and sensing Dee's unease he asked if he could help him. Dee explained the situation and asked if Eddie was or had been in the pub. James said that he'd not seen him since just before nine that morning when he would have been setting off for work. Seeing Dee's disappointment, James explained that he was the landlord; he advised him not to worry and promised that he'd tell Eddie to phone him if and when he turned up. Dee thanked James and left the building. Outside he looked at his phone to see the time. It was a quarter past eight and so knowing there was no reason to stay, Dee returned to the caravan, collected his guitar and cans of lager, switched off the radio and then slowly made his way home. As he neared the top of Long Lane, he met Hetty just setting off to take Albert for a walk. She shone her torch in his direction. "Good evening," she said brightly.

"Oh, yeah, hello."

Hetty stopped walking. "Are you alright, young man? You sound proper fed up."

"Yeah, I'm alright just disappointed, I suppose. Disappointed, confused and, well, let down."

"Oh dear. Want to tell me why?"

"Yeah," Glad to have someone to share his dilemma with, Dee explained.

"Well, I must admit that does sound odd. I mean, young Eddie doesn't know many people here, does he? Having said that I know he mixes with the youngsters in the pub but I can't see as he'd have gone off somewhere else, especially if he'd arranged to meet you and possibly Drake."

"And he hasn't driven anywhere," reasoned Dee, "because his Golf's still there. What's more, his phone is in the caravan and he's not locked up or switched off the radio."

"And James has not seen him either?"

"No."

"Very odd. I'd mention it to your…umm…"

"Dave," said Dee, "I call Mum's bloke Dave. He insists."

"Yes, well, I'd mention it to him and see what he thinks. After all he is a detective so he might be able to come up with a good piece of advice."

"You're right. I'll do that and thanks for listening."

"You're very welcome, young man and I hope your friend turns up soon. I've only chatted to him once but he seemed a very nice lad."

"He is and thank you." Dee continued on his way back to Hillside and Hetty resumed her walk down Long Lane. Half way down, she stopped. "Sorry, Albert, but walkies is curtailed this evening as I need to discuss something with Auntie Lottie."

Lottie was surprised to see Hetty back so soon. "Is it raining, Het? You've only been gone fifteen minutes."

Hetty removed Albert's lead and then her coat. "No, it'd stopped before I went out and it wasn't really much more than drizzle anyway. The reason I'm back though is because I've just been chatting to the young lad from next door."

"What the oik?"

Hetty tutted. "He's not an oik, Lottie. He seems a very nice young man."

"Humph! You've changed your tune."

"Yes and I have good reason. Anyway, one should never judge a book by its cover."

# Chapter Nine

On Tuesday morning, Dolly and Eve were surprised when Eddie had not arrived for work by opening time. Assuming he'd overslept they opened up expecting him to turn up at any minute. When he still had not arrived half an hour later they were concerned and so Dolly rang his mobile. It was answered by James, who because of Dee's concern the previous evening, had gone to Eddie's caravan after closing time to see if he had returned and to pass on Dee's message. Finding the caravan empty, he was troubled and so had returned again in the morning hoping to find him back. It was while he was in the caravan that Dolly rang. Confused and anxious, James explained that Eddie seemed to have vanished and had been missing since the previous evening.

Throughout the day, James, Ella and the Crown and Anchor staff asked its clientele if they had seen Eddie, and at the pasty shop Dolly and Eve did likewise. By the end of the day because no-one had heard from or seen him at all, James, extremely concerned for the lad's safety, rang the police and reported him missing.

On Wednesday morning, Sally Oliver left her husband, Robert soundly sleeping in their flat above the charity shop and made her way down to the beach for her early morning swim. It was something she had done for many years but at her previous address in Birmingham the activity had taken place at a pool not far from their home.

When she and Robert had moved to Cornwall in 2019, Sally was apprehensive about swimming in the sea. Not because she was afraid of the waves or the fact there would be no-one around; it was the temperature of the water that sourced her doubt. For although the morning air might be warm when the sun rose, the water always struck her as cold and she wasn't surprised to learn that the difference in the sea's temperature between winter and summer was only a few degrees.

The morning was dull and there was a nip in the September air as Sally stepped onto the shingle and cast her eyes along the beach in both directions. As was often the case, it was deserted except for a few gulls and a cat sitting on steps leading up to the cliff path. After reaching her favourite spot she quickly removed her clothing and placed each item neatly on one of several benches. Braving the cold in just her swimsuit, she then walked towards the water's edge rubbing her arms to dispel goose pimples. As she dipped her toes into the cold, tumbling water something caught her eye. Something dark, being tossed around on the waves. Blinking to adjust her vision for her spectacles were with her clothing, she managed to focus on the object. When its identity became apparent, she gasped with such force it caused her to cough. Praying she was wrong and that the object was not a body, she stepped into the water oblivious of the cold and swam towards the floating object. When she reached it she cried out in despair. She was right. It was a body. The body of a young man and having heard that Eddie from the pasty shop was missing she didn't doubt for one minute who he was. Holding her breath she clutched the sleeve of his hoodie and swam with him to the shore. Her stomach churned and glad she had not yet had breakfast she dragged him up onto the sand, thankful the tide was ebbing. Without drying herself or dressing she pulled on her shoes and then ran home to her flat to ring the emergency services.

News of Eddie's death had reached all corners of Pentrillick by the end of the day and no-one was more shocked than Hetty, who having heard of Eddie's mysterious disappearance first hand from Dee on Monday evening, felt the loss deeply. She was told of Eddie's misfortune by Debbie, who rang with the news having heard it from her husband, Gideon. Gideon worked with Sally Oliver's husband, Robert, at Pentrillick House where they both had part-time jobs in the gardens and had become good friends.

"Well, it seems cut and dried to me," said Kitty, who had called in after hearing the news in the village. "The poor, poor lad must have gone for a dip and got into trouble. The sea sometimes takes even the most confident swimmers by surprise. It's very sad though, very sad."

Hetty was not convinced. "It's dreadfully sad, I agree, Kitty, but your theory doesn't make sense. He appears to have disappeared on Monday night and was due to meet up with Dee so why on earth would he suddenly go for a swim? It was a dull damp night too so the conditions weren't very inviting."

"Probably thought he had time before Dee arrived," reasoned Kitty, "and as regards the weather, it doesn't really matter once you're in the water. That's what Sally says anyway and I've never known a more dedicated swimmer than her."

"True, I suppose. Dee said they were due to meet at half past seven and so with the pasty shop closing at half five there would be an hour or so to spare."

Lottie shook her head. "But if that's the case why did he not lock the caravan, take his phone and switch off his music, the lights and so forth?"

"Goodness knows," said Hetty, "but out of interest does anyone know what he was wearing when Sally found him? I mean, was it normal clothing, swimming trunks, a wetsuit or whatever?"

"Kitty shook her head. "No idea."

"It's an interesting point though," said Lottie, "and I suppose we'll find out in due course."


On Thursday morning, Debbie down in the village dropping off donations to the charity shop was told the latest news by Daisy who was on duty with Maisie. They in turn had been told by Tess who worked at the Crown and Anchor and had called in with the news following her shift on the bar the previous evening during which the police had called to notify James and Ella of the latest developments. According to the police, the cause of Eddie's death was drowning, therefore he was alive when he went into the sea. When found he was wearing jeans, a T-shirt and a hooded top; the pathology report stated he had been in the water for approximately thirty-six hours. There was bruising on his back, shoulders and ankles and he had a few broken bones. For this reason the powers that be concluded that he must have slipped into the sea somewhere along the coastal path and hit rocks as he fell. The case was therefore likely to be recorded as unexplained. However, because he had arranged to meet Dee Osbourne that evening and there were recently purchased snacks and alcohol in his caravan to back up the claim, it was decided that the case should remain open a little longer on the off-chance any evidence proving otherwise might come to light. After the police left the Crown and Anchor, known facts mingled with speculation, did the rounds and its clientele formed their own opinions as to what happened on Monday evening

Having no reason to rush home because her husband was again at Pentrillick House working in the gardens, Debbie, whose head was full of thoughts and theories, hurried straight to Primrose Cottage hoping to be the first to convey the latest news to Hetty and Lottie.

"There's something not right here," Hetty muttered, "As I said the other day, why would he be anywhere near the sea when he was planning to meet Dee and Drake in his caravan. It doesn't make sense."

"I agree," said Debbie, "there's no reason for him to be out there at all, especially when it was getting dark."

"Would it have been dark then?" Hetty asked, "I mean, we don't know what time he fell from the cliff."

"Well, the sun sets around half sevenish and that was the time he was due to meet Dee so it'd still be light," reasoned Lottie, "but whatever the time was I can't see why he'd be out there in the first place."

"Perhaps he got a call from someone asking him to meet them," suggested Debbie, "and he nipped out quickly intending to be back before Dee arrived."

Hetty shook her head. "No, I don't think that's very likely. Remember, he left the radio on and didn't lock up. I'm sure had he gone out he'd have been more security conscious than that. He left his phone as well. Young people always have their phones with them."

"But he could have left the place unlocked if he thought he'd only be gone for a few minutes," reasoned Debbie, "I mean, there would hardly be anyone on the field snooping around."

"Good point," agreed Lottie, "and if he did go out to meet someone on say the beach he'd have taken a short cut through the hedge at the back of the pub field onto the cliff path."

"I think you might be onto something there," conceded Hetty, "because if that was the case he could well have tripped or slipped there and tumbled into the sea, especially if he was in a hurry. Which of course is what the police assume happened. Him falling, I mean."

"Which makes it an accident then," said Debbie.

"Well I hope it was. I'd hate to think of someone taking the life of the poor lad." Lottie looked relieved.

"No, no, no," Hetty shook her head, "It can't be the case, can it? Because if he had gone to meet someone on the beach then that someone would have seen what happened to him and reported it."

"Not if Eddie was already in the water when whoever he was going to meet got there," said Debbie, "Because I've just remembered, according to Maisie, Tess said it was stated by someone in the pub that it would have been high tide around then and the sea was quite choppy. So if there was no sign of Eddie, the person in question would just have assumed he hadn't turned up and gone off home."

"But if he was to meet someone, then that person would surely have come forward to say about it even if the meeting hadn't taken place. I mean everyone in the village was aware Eddie was missing. You'd have to be a hermit or deaf not to have heard about it." Feeling flustered, Hetty unbuttoned her cardigan and rolled up its sleeves.

"Interesting observation," said Lottie, "because that means said person might be keeping mum because he or she is either responsible for his death or is covering up for someone else."

Debbie gasped. "Which would mean it wasn't an accident."

Hetty slowly and thoughtfully tapped the arm of her chair. "It's just a thought, but might Eddie have disturbed a burglar in his caravan? If so, the burglar might on hearing Eddie arrive back, have hidden in say, the bedroom or somewhere like that. Eddie would then have gone in, put his purchases on the table along with his phone and switched on the lights and radio as usual. The burglar then realising he needed to get away, could have run for the door when Eddie's back was turned. If so, Eddie might have seen him from the corner of his eye and given chase and they ended up on the cliff path."

"Good theory, Het," acknowledged Lottie, "except for one thing. As far as we know the lock wasn't broken so if someone had already been there he or she would have needed a key to the caravan."

"You're right," Hetty looked at the clock. "I think we need a trip to the pub to see what we can pick up. Tess is sure to know what the key situation is."

"No good going until evening," said Lottie, "because I doubt Tess will be there before six at the earliest."

"In which case we'll pop down around sevenish."

"You can count me in," said Debbie, "and perhaps we could ask Margot to join us too. Be good to pick her brains. That's assuming David tells her what he's up to."

Hetty shook her head. "But if he does she'll not tell us. It's a good idea though but I think it best if we act cool and maybe get to question her, subtly of course, over the garden fence or something like that."


After lunch, Hetty and Lottie left Primrose Cottage to take Albert for a walk. As Lottie closed the front door, a van approached from further along Blackberry Way. As it passed by the two men inside nodded, waved and smiled at the sisters.

"Well they seem like nice chaps," Hetty was easily won over by a friendly smile. "I suppose they've just been home for lunch."

"I agree," chuckled Lottie, "and I must admit I like the slogan for their business even if it is rather corny."

"Oh. I didn't notice it," confessed Hetty. "What did it say?"

"Jude and Den, the window gleaming men."

Hetty closed the gates. "Oh dear."

At the bottom of Long Lane the sisters turned right; walked past the Crown and Anchor and the village school and then turned into a narrow lane. The lane took them up-hill past a care home for the elderly and led towards the opening into Cobblestone Close. As they reached the Close entrance they saw Emma, Lottie's grandson Zac's fiancée, waving to them as she strode along the pavement in their direction. They stopped and waited until she reached them.

"Glad to have seen you," said Emma, "because I'm sure you'll be delighted to hear that we're adding two new categories to next year's Pentrillick in Bloom competition."

"You reckon everything will be okay and it'll go ahead then?" Hetty had her doubts.

"Oh yes. Tristen, Samantha and I had a brief meeting this morning at Pentrillick House along with James and Ella and other business owners and we decided unanimously that it must go ahead for the sake of sanity if nothing else. We're going to be flexible with the date of the judging though just in case things flare up but everyone will get plenty of warning."

"A wise decision," said Hetty, approvingly, "and something to look forward to next year."

"I'm surprised James and Ella were at the meeting so soon after the news of Eddie's death," said Lottie.

"I know. Poor James. Tristan did suggest we postpone it but James insisted it went ahead. He said right now, we all need something positive in our lives. I must admit he was far from his normal jovial self though."

"I bet he was. Anyway, what are these new categories, Emma?" Lottie asked.

"One is vegetables and the other is a themed garden. The vegetables can be grown in tubs, in gardens or even on allotments, and the themed garden can be absolutely anything."

"What a good idea. I know a lot of people turned to gardening during the lockdowns and veg seemed a firm favourite. We even thought about turning the end of our garden into a veg plot, didn't we, Het?"

"We did and now there's a category for it we'll definitely do it next year. Not so sure about a themed garden though but it should appeal to the creative."

"So, can we tell people or is it a secret for now?" Lottie was longing to tell Debbie and Kitty.

"Go ahead, it's not a secret so tell as many as you can. In fact the more the merrier. We're in the throes of making posters and will get them distributed in the next couple of days. We want to give people plenty of time as, like you they'll probably want to redesign their gardens."

"You must tell Bill," said Hetty to her sister.

"He already knows," said Emma, "I rang Zac as soon as we'd decided to go ahead and he passed the news on. Needless to say his dad is thrilled to bits and already planning his contribution." Emma chuckled: "I think a large part of the lawn might be under threat."

After saying their goodbyes, Emma set off down the hill towards the village and the sisters continued their walk up the hill. As they neared the top they met a young woman alone. She wore ripped jeans, a baggy T-shirt and flip-flops. Her face was devoid of make-up and her long hair was piled up in an untidy bun. Because she looked familiar both greeted her with a smile but to their dismay their greeting was rebuffed. The young woman tossed her head and continued her walk with her nose in the air.

"Humph," grunted Hetty, "Who do you reckon she is?"

"No idea but, if I had to guess I'd say she's probably the Hamilton girl."

"Do you think so?" Hetty turned to watch the young woman as she disappeared round a bend in the road, "You could be right but she doesn't look anything like she did in the pub the other night. Having said that, I couldn't see her very well because she had her back to us."

"And she was all dolled up then. Anyway, if it is her she's called Serena and perhaps she's just having a bad day," said Lottie, kindly. "It can't be easy being young in this day and age, especially when your family is a household name."

"But surely it's no more difficult being young today than it was for us."

"Oh but it is, Het. Think about it. With social media, mobile phones, and stuff I've no idea about, it must be a nightmare. There's too much pressure and emphasis on keeping up with the Joneses, looking perfect and so forth. I'd hate to be young today."

"Maybe, but it'd be nice to be a few years younger than we are. I mean, yuck, we'll be seventy next year and the media haven't helped during this Covid business. They seem to think everyone over sixty has one foot in the grave."

Lottie smiled. "They do and I must admit that does get me down. I wouldn't mind being a bit younger. Say fifty-nine instead of sixty-nine."

"Make it forty-nine and I'll agree."

When they reached the end of the road at the top of the hill they turned round and retraced their steps. On arriving back in the village they walked along the main street to the shop to get a bag of flour. As they passed the charity shop on their way back, Maisie caught Lottie's eye and beckoned them inside.

"We've just heard something that we're sure you'd like to know," gushed Maisie before they had time to close the shop door.

"Hetty's eyes flashed. "We're all ears."

"I thought you would be. Do you want to tell them, Daisy or shall I?"

"You do it. You're better at recalling facts than I am. Not that there's a great deal to remember."

"Okay, well it's about young Eddie and it's Marlene who told us. She's just been in, you see, with some clothes her kids no longer wear. Anyway, a day or two before Eddie was last seen alive, Marlene was walking along the pavement by the pub field and she saw a girl on the field hiding amongst the shrubbery. She didn't recognise her and thought nothing of it, but then a couple of days later, when she heard that Eddie was missing, she wondered if he was on social media and so out of curiosity searched his name hoping to learn something about him. She found him easily enough and one of the things she discovered was that he'd recently split up with his girlfriend. She then clicked onto the girlfriend's name and read a month-old post saying how upset she was about the parting because she thought they'd get married. There were no posts after that and that's probably because according to friends she'd gone into hiding and none of them knew where she was."

Hetty's jaw dropped. "So Marlene thinks the girl she saw might have been the ditched girlfriend."

"Precisely."

"And," Daisy added, "we're wondering if she might have something to do with his death."

"Any idea of her name?" Lottie asked.

"Her Christian name's Willow," said Maisie, "and Marlene thinks her surname was Mackenzie."

"We must check her out when we get home," said Hetty.

Maisie shook her head. "I'm afraid you can't. After the body was discovered and identified as Eddie, Marlene tried to look up the girlfriend again but her account, and Eddie's, are both now deactivated and so there's nothing to see."

"Has Marlene told the police?" Lottie asked.

"Yes, but whether or not anything will come of it we'll have to wait and see."

In the evening as planned, and intrigued by the latest developments, Hetty and Lottie met up with Debbie at the Crown and Anchor. However, it was quiet and there was no-one from whom to glean even the tiniest piece of information. Jackie didn't know whether or not there was a spare key to the caravan and all agreed it would be insensitive to ask James. To add insult to injury, Tess was not in as it was her night off.

# Chapter Ten

On Friday the weather was bright and sunny, and so Hetty changed her bed and cleaned her room. As she straightened the cushions on her ottoman, she noticing her windows looked grubby and so decided to clean them as well. The inside she did with ease but the outside was always a tricky affair as it meant hanging on to the window frame while she leaned out. As she stretched as far as possible to reach the top corner, Jude Sharpe turned into Blackberry Way, whistling happily with hands tucked in the pockets of his jeans. When he saw Hetty he raised his hands in horror and shouted. "Go back in. You could fall."

Hetty did as she was told but looking down assured Jude she was perfectly safe having done the same manoeuvre many times before.

"It doesn't look safe to me. Please stay there. Don't move." He then ran along the road to Fuchsia Cottage to return minutes later with the ladder from the top of the works' van. With haste he put the ladder against the wall just below the window and climbed up. "Come on, now pass me your cleaning things."

Hetty, amused at being bossed around, obeyed. Jude then cleaned the windows until they shone.

"I've not seen you close up before but I assume you're one of the window cleaning lads from Fuchsia Cottage."

"At your service, ma'am." He winked.

"In which case I must pay you."

"Oh, no you won't, as far as I'm concerned, it's a neighbourly thing to do. Besides it's not often I get to come to the rescue of a damsel in distress." He held out his hand. "Jude Sharpe at your service."

"Delighted to meet you, Jude. I'm Henrietta Tonkins but everyone calls me Hetty." They shook hands.

"Delighted to meet you too and while I'm here I'll do the other upstairs windows."

"Bless you and when you've done that you must come in for a cup of tea and a slice of apple pie."

"Yummy, I'd like that. I'm on my own today because we've taken the day off so Dennis can play golf and the girls are in the shop. I've just been down to see if they need any help since they've lost poor Eddie but they're both fine."

"Yes, very sad. Dolly and Eve must be devastated."

"They are. Both got along with him really well. Goodness knows what's behind his death. I just hope for his mum's sake it was an accident and not…well, you know."

"Likewise," Hetty rubbed over a smear she'd made on the inside of the window, "It's probably a bit indelicate to ask so soon after his death but did he ever mention a girlfriend?"

"Only briefly. Dolly asked him if he had a girl back home and he said not any more. He ended his most recent relationship just before he came down here because the girl in question was always dropping hints about getting married. He didn't want that. Said he wanted to make a career for himself and then maybe settle down when he's in his mid to late thirties."

"I see." Not wanting to say why she'd asked, Hetty quickly changed the subject and said she would pop downstairs to open the front door and that he was to come in when he was ready. She then left Jude to clean the other windows and after opening the door for him, went into the

71

sitting room to relay the news to Lottie who was sewing new buttons on her favourite cardigan having lost one of the original set.

When the windows were cleaned and Jude was seated in the living room with the sisters, Lottie watched him as he happily talked of his family and told a little about himself. He was slightly built, had sandy coloured hair and a few freckles across the bridge of his nose. His smile was warm and his voice melodious. After Hetty said she'd not seen his brother, Dennis other than when he'd driven by in the van, she asked if they looked alike.

"Sadly not," chuckled Jude, "Dennis is taller than me, fitter and stronger built too. His hair is dark although there are signs of grey around his ears and I suppose all in all he's the epitome of tall, dark and handsome." He took out his phone, scrolled down his pictures and showed one of Dennis to the sisters, "Mind you," he added, "he's also very temperamental where as I'm level-headed, placid and easy to get on with."


Later in the day, Norman Williams peeped in the kitchen where Jackie Paige was preparing the evening meal inside their home at Cobblestone Close. "I'm just popping down to the village hall, Jackie. I haven't been there for a week or more so I'd better check all is okay."

Jackie looked up from the pan where she stirred a mustard sauce. "Alright, Norm. Dinner should be ready around sevenish."

"Ideal. I'll be back long before then."

Jackie was Norman's twenty four year old lodger. Previously they had been next-door neighbours in Dawlish where Jackie lived with her parents and Norman lived with his elderly widowed mother. They became good friends when Jackie and her mother helped Norman to look after his mother in the last months of her life. It was after his mother's death that Norman looked into his past and Jackie who had an interest in ancestry had helped him. This led them to Cornwall where Norman discovered his roots and eventually decided to retire to Pentrillick, the village of his birth. Because Jackie had made friends in the village during their visit she asked if she might go with him as a paying lodger and Norman readily agreed.

They moved into the house on the new estate in 2019 just before Christmas and straight away Jackie secured a job at the Crown and Anchor where she assisted the chef or worked on the bar. Norman meanwhile, who had a few years to go before he received his state pension, decided to do a bit of painting and decorating. It was something he enjoyed and was good at. However, during the first lockdown work soon dried up and so he was glad when he saw the job of caretaker for the village hall advertised for no other reason than it'd give him something to do.

As Norman arrived at the village hall he saw Lottie's son Bill walking in his direction along the pavement with Crumpet, the Bakehouse family dog. Not having seen each other for a while they stopped to chat and put the world to rights.

"Before I forget. Would you be interested in doing a little painting job for us, Norman? There's no rush but the paint on the outside of the three upstairs back windows is flaking and Sandra keeps nagging me to get it sorted before the bad weather sets in. She's even bought the paint, brushes and new sandpaper. I've told her I really don't have the time but if I'm honest it's because I don't really have a head for heights, especially while standing on a ladder. We'll obviously pay you the going rate."

"Of course I'll do it and I don't want payment either. You and Sandra have been very good to me over the few years and one good turn deserves another."

"Well, we'll see about that."

When Bill left to continue his walk, the church clock struck seven. Realising he was going to be late for dinner, Norman quickly opened up the hall, gave the main room a cursory glance, locked the door again and then hurriedly made his way home to Cobblestone Close.

# Chapter Eleven

The following day, the police rang James to say that Eddie's caravan and the surrounding area was no longer a crime scene and that an officer would be along shortly to remove the police tapes. After the officer had been, James walked across the pub field and locked up the caravan until Eddie's next of kin were able to visit Cornwall and gather together his belongings.

Two days later, Eddie's mother arrived by train. Her husband had offered to escort her but she said she wanted to be alone and have time to think. For her husband although she loved him dearly was not Eddie's father. Eddie's father had died five years earlier following a heart attack.

James as pre-arranged on the phone met her at Penzance station and then drove her back to Pentrillick. Her original plan was to pack Eddie's possessions into his Golf and then leave that same day, but Ella, seeing she looked tired, persuaded her to stay the night as their guest rather than make the long drive home. After weighing up the situation she agreed, saying she was emotionally drained. It was as she locked Eddie's car and walked across the field that she realised she had not seen his mouth organ. Knowing it was his prize possession, a gift from his grandmother on his twenty-first birthday, and sure he would have had it with him in Cornwall, she returned to the caravan and searched thoroughly but to no avail. Wondering if he might have taken it into the pub for some reason and left it there, she went in to ask James and

Ella. James said that while Eddie was often in the pub, usually playing pool, he had never played any musical instruments inside the premises but that he, Ella, and the staff would keep a look out for it nevertheless. Whereupon, Eddie's mother conceded that maybe it was still in his room back in Sheffield. Jackie, who was clearing tables in the bar, heard what was said and told them Eddie did have the instrument with him in Cornwall because he was playing it one evening when she arrived for work. He was sitting on the steps of his caravan at the time and the tune he played, much to her surprise, was her father's favourite, 'Amazing Grace'.

The police, much like Pentrillick's ladies, continued their inquiries into Eddie Madigan's death. For although their original assumption was that he must have accidently fallen from the cliffs, certain facts made it look improbable. Eddie was a fit and healthy young man. Were he to have met his death shortly before Dee Osborne arrived at the caravan then it would still have been light, and the cliff path, although uneven in parts, was a safe enough passage for anyone who was sure-footed. Therefore it was felt by many working on the case that they needed to look further into the possibility of foul play. After much discussion the most obvious theory was that Eddie was pushed after having walked out onto the cliffs, for whatever reason, through a gap in the hedge at the back of the pub's field. If this were the case then a scuffle with an unknown person might well have ensued or perhaps he was taken unawares by someone he knew and trusted. However, due to recent rain, a thorough search of that area showed no trace of identifiable footprints. Neither were there any other forms of forensic evidence.

House to house enquiries had backed up the statement made by Dee Osbourne that Eddie proposed to purchase alcohol from the shop on his way back to his caravan. For part of the way he was escorted by the Burton twins, Kate and Vicki and several people saw them walking along the main street together including Mr and Mrs Haddock in the fish and chip shop who waved to them as they passed by. An interview with the proprietors of the convenience store confirmed cans of lager and a bottle of vodka were purchased by the deceased at 17.48 along with two packets of peanuts and curry flavoured crisps.

Details of calls made and received on Eddie's phone, left in the caravan, established that the last call received was from Dee Osborne and no other calls had been made or received since midday when he had phoned his mother. This meant he had not phoned Drake Hamilton as he had indicated he would to ask him to join himself and Dee for a few beers. On the off-chance that Eddie might have briefly called at Sea view Cottage before he bumped into the twins on his way home from the pasty shop to speak to Drake in person, officers called at the cottage but Drake had not seen or spoken to Eddie since the previous weekend when they had been out fishing together at Marazion.

Following the discovery of Eddie's body, Eve and Dolly at the pasty shop had been interviewed and they confirmed that Eddie had left the shop at closing time and as instructed had set the alarm and posted the keys through the shop's letterbox.

At the Crown and Anchor, police questioned James Dale who had reported Eddie missing the day after he was last seen. They also questioned Gibson Bailey, a guest at the establishment, and Tess Dobson who saw Eddie walking towards his caravan on the day he disappeared as she arrived at the pub early for her shift starting at half past six. However they were unable to find any witnesses who had seen him in the vicinity of the coastline or anywhere else after Tess saw him going towards his caravan. A few in the force emphatically believed his death was an accident and DI Bray would have agreed were it not for the fact that there were no fingerprints on his mobile phone nor on any of the surfaces in the caravan, other than those of James Dale, the Crown and Anchor's landlord, who had gone to the caravan hoping to find Eddie home; which indicated someone at some point had wiped the phone and surfaces clean. Furthermore, Eddie Madigan's mouth organ was missing.

"I think we need to look into this opera singer's credentials," said Hetty, as they watched the six o'clock news, "because I reckon he's a phony and if you remember, Tess Googled his name after he arrived but couldn't find any reference to him."

"Maybe he's not that well known then. Not everyone's name is on the internet. Anyway, why do you think that all of a sudden?"

Hetty shrugged her shoulders. "Don't know really, but that bloke in the last news story reminded me of him and that's why he's on my mind."

"What!" gasped Lottie, "You mean the chap talking to a reporter at the airport? He looked nothing like the opera singer."

"Yes, but I didn't say he looked like him just that he reminded me of him. Anyway, as regards Gibson Bailey being a phoney, it's just a feeling I get. I mean he doesn't look like an opera singer, does he? He's too chubby. Although I suppose the excess weight he carries is quite the norm."

"Well, I rather like him," said Lottie, "Not that I've seen much of him. I know he's fond of walking though because Kitty said she'd seen him on several occasions when out walking herself and he's always polite and greets her warmly. He likes taking pictures too and usually has a camera with him."

"Hmm, what sort of pictures?" Hetty wondered if photography might in any way be incriminating evidence.

"No idea, although Kitty said he was taking pictures of the sea from the cliff path the other day so perhaps he's partial to seascapes."

"Or sea birds, but whatever, I intend to interrogate him when I get the chance."

"Well if you go to the pub tonight you go on your own because there are a couple of programmes on the telly I want to watch."

However, the following evening, Hetty was able to persuade Lottie to visit the Crown and Anchor by promising to do the washing up every day for a week. She considered it a small price to pay for the opportunity to suss out the opera singer, should he still be in Cornwall. To her delight he was not only still in residence but was sitting all alone at his usual table in the corner. In front of him was a glass of whisky and his mobile phone. He was reading a book.

After a glass of wine, Hetty stood and made her way to the Ladies. On her way back she stopped near to the singer's table. "I see you're reading Richard Osman's novel. I've considered buying it. Is it any good?"

Gibson Bailey looked up. "I'm enjoying it very much but then I suppose it wouldn't be to everyone's taste."

"A bit like music, I suppose." Hetty smiled sweetly, delighted to have brought up the subject with such ease.

"Very much so."

"And you I believe are an opera singer. That must be very rewarding."

"It is, or should I say, was. Not been doing much of it lately but hope to get back into the swing of things by the end of the month."

"And very nice too." Hetty glanced at her sister and wondered if she could hear their conversation, "One of my favourite opera singers is Leonardo Riccioni."

"Very wise of you. He does have a wonderful voice but seldom sings now, which is a shame."

"Do you know him?"

"Not personally but I have many of his recordings and have watched him perform on several occasions over the years."

Hetty returned to her seat, a triumphant look on her face. "He's a fake."

"Who's a fake?"

"Gibson Bailey of course. Didn't you see me talking to him?"

"Well, yes but…"

Hetty sat down. "I brought up the subject of opera and said my favourite singer is Leonardo Riccioni."

"Who?"

"Exactly. I made the name up but Mr Phoney over there fell in my trap and said Leonardo Riccioni has a wonderful voice and it's a shame he doesn't sing much now."

"Hmm, that's interesting. Perhaps we will have to keep an eye on him then."

When Hetty saw Tess collecting empty glasses from the next table she suddenly remembered to ask about a spare key to Eddie's caravan. To her delight, Tess said there was a spare and that it was kept on a hook by the phone inside the kitchen. Hetty didn't need to explain why she had asked; Tess put two and two together and said the police had already asked the same question and that they had told them as far as they knew the key had not moved from its hook.

"Maybe not," whispered Hetty, as Tess returned to the bar with the glasses, "but with Gibson staying in the pub, he could have returned it before anyone saw it was missing."

"But why would Gibson break into Eddie's caravan?" Lottie asked, "I mean, it would hardly have been to pinch stuff."

"I don't know but it's certainly food for thought."

After two glasses of wine and with mission accomplished, the sisters were ready to go home but as they reached for their coats, Debbie and Gideon arrived.

"Oh, don't go," said Gideon, "I've not seen you two for ages although I know through Debs what you're up to most of the time."

"In that case we must stay and force down another glass of wine." Hetty reached for her handbag: "the drinks are on me, folks."

Lottie, feeling she'd had enough wine, asked for an orange juice. Debbie opted for chardonnay and Gideon a bitter lemon. Hetty, repeating the requests beneath her breath, lest she forget, went to the bar, but in order to weaken her alcohol level, she bought herself a glass of soda water to drink between sips of wine.

A little later, she was in need of a second trip to the Ladies. It was as she returned she spotted their new neighbours, David and Margot in the corner. Glad to see them she smiled and asked how they were. As they responded a voice spoke from behind.

"Miss Tonkins. How nice to see you. It's been a while, hasn't it?"

Hetty turned to see the person who had spoken standing behind with three drinks on a tray. "Oh, Detective Inspector Fox. What a surprise. How lovely to see you."

"Do you two know each other?" Margot asked.

"Oh yes. The paths of Miss Tonkins and her delightful sister Mrs Burton have crossed mine many times over the past few years."

The eyebrows of David and Margot rose in unison.

Hetty felt her face flush. "So umm do you two work together?"

DI Fox shook his head. "No, Dave here is my replacement. I've retired from the force now."

"Really! But surely you're not old enough to retire."

"No, not quite but I've retired for health reasons. I'm a widower now and lost my wife just over a year ago. Sadly it's affected my ability to concentrate and think straight," he placed the tray on the table and sat down, "but you still might see me around as I'm thinking of moving to the village and doing a bit of painting. Artwork, that is, not walls and ceilings. I have a passion for painting small boats."

"Oh, that's nice but I'm sorry to hear about your wife." Hoping Dave and Margot would ask no more questions of her previous encounters with the retired inspector, Hetty looked at her watch, "Oh, good heavens, is that the time? I must dash. Nice to have seen you again Inspector. I'll leave you all to enjoy the rest of the evening."

Her face flushed, Hetty scuttled off back to her sister and their friends to assimilate what she had learned and relay the news.


"So how come you know Hetty and Lottie?" Margot asked as Hetty disappeared round the corner.

"DI Fox chuckled. "They, along with their two friends have a habit of getting involved with local crimes and for that reason I've interviewed them on several occasions."

"You mean, they're amateur sleuths?" David looked shocked.

"I'm afraid so and I should imagine right now they're deep into finding out just what happened to young Eddie Madigan."

David Bray groaned.

Relieved to get back to Lottie, Debbie and Gideon, Hetty fanned her flushed face and told of her embarrassing encounter. Gideon chuckled; Lottie and Debbie sympathised.

"We've a bit of news for you too," said Lottie, "Just listen to what Debbie and Gideon have to say."

"I'm all ears," said Hetty, glad of a change of subject.

Debbie put down her drink. "Well, I meant to tell you when we got here as it's the reason we called in, on the off-chance that you'd be here, that is. But before I got the chance to mention it you started telling us about your chat with the opera chappie and I was so mesmerised it pushed it from my mind. Anyway, the thing is, Gideon and I have just been to Penzance to try out the food in a new restaurant that opened up last week, and as we were walking back to the car we saw Dennis Sharpe and he was not alone. Hanging onto his arm was a woman, tall and slim, with blonde, obviously bleached, hair but she was beautifully made-up, so as you can tell by the description, it wasn't Dolly."

Hetty's mouth dropped. "So, who was she?"

"No idea, but she looked older than him. In her mid-fifties, I'd say." As Debbie spoke, James rang the bell for last orders.

"Right," said Hetty, "this calls for action. I suggest we meet at Primrose Cottage tomorrow morning at eleven o'clock prompt for a meeting."

Gideon chuckled. "You lot are priceless."

# Chapter Twelve

At eleven o'clock promptly, Debbie pulled up in the driveway of Primrose Cottage and hurried into the house where Hetty, having heard the car, stood with front door open to greet her. Kitty was already seated at the table in the sitting room having been informed earlier of the meeting by Lottie as soon as she considered it to be a socially acceptable time to make a phone call.

"Right, who wants to take notes?" Before she sat, Hetty placed a notebook and pen on the table alongside a tray brimming with refreshment.

"I'll do it," said Debbie, "I like writing but it's something I seldom do these days with keypads and keyboards for everything." With pen in hand, Debbie asked for the first subject matter.

"Suspects," gushed Hetty, "we need to get them written down so that we can analyse them in great detail. And top of the list must be Dennis Sharpe."

Debbie wrote down Dennis's name. "Right, done, so who's next?"

Kitty raised her hand. "I think we ought to list everyone who's new to the area including visitors and then we can eliminate them one by one."

"Good idea," agreed Hetty, "and so after Dennis add Gibson Bailey."

"I can't believe you still think he might have nicked the spare key and broken into the caravan, Het," snapped Lottie. "The notion of Gibson hiding somewhere and trying to creep out while Eddie's back was turned is too daft for words."

Hetty peered over the rim of her reading glasses. "Truth is stranger than fiction, Lottie."

"I'll add him for now because we can always cross him off later," Wanting to keep the peace, Debbie scribbled down Gibson's name.

Lottie nodded. "Fair enough."

"And I suppose as we already have Dennis down we must include Dolly, Eve and Jude too as they're all new to the area." Debbie added the three names.

"And the Haddocks," said Kitty.

Debbie laughed. "And we mustn't forget Margo and Dave next door."

"Nor Margot's son, Dee," said Lottie.

"Surely that's it," Debbie laid down the pen.

Hetty shook her head. "Oh, no, you've yet to add the Hamiltons."

With the list complete they then began to delete all unlikely names.

"Well you can cross out Dave and Margot for a start," said Kitty, "They're a lovely couple and with him being a copper it's unlikely he's involved."

"And Dee," said Hetty, "after all he was the one found Eddie was missing."

"True," mused Debbie, "but we only have his word for that. As much as I think it unlikely, he could have made the whole thing up."

Kitty gasped. "Good point but I'm sure you're wrong as he struck me as being a nice lad. I suppose we ought to leave him on, though. Otherwise there will be no-one left."

"I agree, Kitty, and before Lottie starts ranting again, leave Gibson Bailey on too, Debbie. There's something about him that makes me suspicious and as I've already said, him staying in the pub means he was very close to the murder scene."

"Humph," Lottie took in a deep breath to hide her annoyance.

"Alleged murder scene," Debbie reminded them, "After all we don't know whether or not the police think it was murder."

Hetty frowned. "But I thought we'd all agreed it was."

"Yes, we have but the police might not agree."

"That's a minor detail," said Kitty, "Let's get back to the list."

Lottie agreed. "You can cross out the Haddocks, Debbie. I mean, surely they'd not be involved."

"I agree: what's more, they were serving in the shop from four 'til eight and so they'd have umpteen alibis." Debbie crossed out their names.

"How about the Hamiltons then?" asked Hetty. "That Serena looks a right misery, so leave her on."

"Okay, but we'll take Angie off because according to the Haddocks, she's lovely." Debbie crossed out Angie's name. "And we can take out Bentley too because he was friends with Eddie's late father."

"And cross out Drake because he and Eddie were friends and went fishing together recently." Hetty reminded them.

"True, but they could have had an argument over something or other," reasoned Lottie, "so I think he should stay for now."

"Okay," said Debbie, "we'll leave him on."

"Right, so that just leaves the pasty shop lot," said Kitty, "and I think we can rule out the girls."

"And Jude," Hetty had a soft spot for him since he'd cleaned her windows, "but leave Dennis as we're pretty sure he's up to no good."

"So, who does that leave us with?" Kitty asked Debbie.

"Oh dear, only five. Young Dee Osborne, Gibson Bailey, Serena and Drake Hamilton, and Dennis Sharpe."

Hetty tapped her finger nails against her teeth. "Okay, so let's go for motives."

"Well, apart from the fact that any of them might have had an argument with Eddie, I can't think of a single one," sighed Lottie.

Debbie agreed, laid down the pen, took a slice of cake from the tray and bit into it. "Hmm, this is nice. What is it?"

"Hevva cake," said Hetty. "Knowing you were all coming round I nipped down to the pasty shop first thing this morning and bought it to augment Lottie's coffee cake because there wasn't much left."

"Hevva cake! What on earth's that?"

"It's Cornish and the girls have started making it because it's a favourite of Betsy Triggs. Betsy doesn't do any baking now of course so she gave the girls her mother's recipe hoping they'd add it to the shop's list of goodies for sale."

"And they have, but I must admit I've never heard of it." Debbie took another bite.

"Apparently it's a traditional teatime treat which dates back to pilchard fishing days," said Hetty. "Blokes called huers would watch from the clifftops for shoals of pilchards and then signal to the fishermen out in their boats by waving their arms, branches or whatever. When the fish were caught and landed they'd shout 'hevva, hevva' and the fishermen's dutiful wives would pop back home and start baking. Cornish hevva, sometimes known as heavy cake, was a particular favourite of the time."

"Well I never," said Kitty. "I didn't know that and I've lived here all my life."

"Dolly said it sells really well and to show their gratitude they drop a complimentary slice round to Betsy every day at eleven o'clock while it's still warm to have with her morning coffee."

Debbie finished her cake. "Well, I'm pleased to hear that Betsy's being looked after because the likes of her are the salt of the earth."

All three ladies nodded their agreement.

"Anyway, now we've finished the cake discussion, I suggest we get back to the list of motives." Lottie was amazed at how quickly her sister and friends could deviate from the matter in hand. "Not that I can think of any," she added.

"I agree," said Kitty, "and it's more likely to be someone not on the list anyway."

Hetty shook her head. "No, you're all forgetting Dennis. He has a motive. Think about it, ladies. He was spotted in Penzance last night with an unknown blonde, who clearly wasn't his girlfriend, Dolly."

"I don't think we should jump to conclusions because she might even be an older sister," reasoned Lottie.

Kitty shook her head. "No, Dennis and Jude don't have a sister. I know that because it cropped up in a chat we had when they first arrived."

"In which case he's our number one suspect and we need to keep a very close eye on him," Hetty picked up the pen and drew a thick line beneath his name.

"Okay. Let's assume you're right, Het," said Lottie. "What would be his motive for pushing young Eddie off the cliff path?"

"Well, I think it's quite obvious. Eddie, like Debbie and Gideon, must have seen Dennis with the unknown blonde and he threatened to tell Dolly. I mean, if that were the case he'd want to shut him up because he has a nice little number here in Pentrillick, especially with the pasty shop's potential for being a very pleasant house. It'll be worth a fortune when it's done up."

Lottie groaned. "And now I suppose you're going to suggest we follow him everywhere, Het."

"All in good time. First we need to find out through either Jude or the girls where he was supposed to be last night because he certainly wouldn't have told them he was going to meet another woman, would he?"

"And how do we go about that? We can hardly just ask them," said Debbie.

"The moment will arise. Just you wait and see. Meanwhile, we ought not to forget our other suspects and so must keep an eye on them too. In fact, we must keep an eye on everyone."


That same morning, Norman began work on the outside, upstairs windows at the back of the Old Bakehouse. Bill and Sandra were already at work, and just before midday the twins, Vicki and Kate, left for the Crown and Anchor to earn some money waitressing during the lunchtime session. At five past one, Norman's stomach began to rumble, so he locked up and walked along the road to buy himself a pasty. As the weather was fine he decided, rather than take it back to the Old Bakehouse, to sit on a bench alongside the church wall by the bus stop and watch the world go by. As he sat relishing the warmth of the September sunshine, Drake Hamilton appeared himself carrying a pasty. He paused when he saw the bench was taken and sat down on the church steps by the lichgate.

"You're more than welcome to join me," said Norman, "There's plenty of room for two and I don't bite."

"Thanks."

"You're welcome. It's not often I get the chance to sit by a star of stage and screen."

"More like TV ads," laughed Drake.

"You're not in the West End show with your mum and dad then."

"No, although I have done a bit of stage work. As I said I've mostly done adverts although I've got a small part coming up in a TV series soon and so that's why I'm here. We don't start filming until October so I thought I'd make use of my parents' misfortune and enjoy a spell by the sea." Drake took a bite of his pasty.

"Very nice. I'll have to look out for your show when it's broadcast. What's it called?"

"Bridge Cottage and I play the part of Jimmy Blythe."

"Ideal, I'll make a note of that when I get home."

Drake seemed amused. "So do you live here then? In Pentrillick, I mean."

"Yeah, and I wouldn't want to live anywhere else."

"So you're Cornish."

"Yes. In fact I was actually born here in the village but we moved away before I had any memories of the place. When in later years I discovered my roots I decided to come back."

"Lucky you. I could quite happily live and work down here."

"I've heard on the grapevine that you knew the poor lad that drowned. Very sad all that."

"Yeah, it is. I knew him because our dads had been mates for years. Going back to when they started infant school together in fact, and they always kept in touch. I admired Eddie because he played the guitar and started a band. I play too, you see, but I'm not in the same league as he was. The last time I saw him before he came down here was at his dad's funeral. We all went, Mum, Dad, Serena and me. Poor bloke died following a heart attack. Ed's mum was devastated but eventually she met someone else and has recently remarried. Ed said she seems happy and that made him happy too. I never dreamt when we came down here that he'd be here too, and likewise he was surprised to see us. We met up a couple of weeks ago and went fishing." Drake sighed, "I try not to think about what's happened to him. It's all just too horrible."

"It is," Norman tried to cheer Drake up. "So did you ever see him playing in his band, I can't remember the name?"

"Rhubarb Chutney. I saw them a few times in their early days but never got to see them after they sort of made it. I have both their albums though and they're really good."

"So do you still play the guitar?"

Drake laughed. "Only when the mood takes me. Poor Ed. I was really envious when he became well-known. He was doing something he was passionate about, you see and I think it's good to follow your dreams."

"You don't feel the same about acting then?"

"Good heavens, no. Life's too short to spend it pretending to be someone else."

# Chapter Thirteen

Just after eleven, as Hetty picked up the post from the doormat at Primrose Cottage, the doorbell rang. Hetty answered and standing outside was Gibson Bailey.

"Good morning, dear. Tess told me where you lived and I've brought something for you," he held up his copy of the Richard Osman book he had been reading in the pub, "I've finished it now and because you showed interest in it, I thought rather than take it home with me I'd pass it on to you. I hope you don't mind."

Hetty took the book from him. "Mind, why would I mind?"

"Well, you know, this Covid thing. Some people are very fussy and I thought you might not want to handle it."

Hetty laughed. "I'll risk it and thank you very much."

"You're welcome," He turned to leave.

"I take it you're going home then."

"Yes, I am. Duty calls but I've enjoyed my stay albeit briefer than I'd anticipated."

"I'm sorry about that. Any news as to whether or not the Hamiltons will be off soon?"

Gibson shrugged his shoulders. "Not as far as I know. Last time I spoke to Angie she said they'd had no luck with another theatre and so are waiting for the repairs to be made."

"That's good...I mean, what a shame." Hetty smiled sweetly and after she'd waved Gibson goodbye she closed the door. "It'll be a real nuisance if any more of our suspects decide to go home," she muttered.

"Our suspects," laughed Lottie, overhearing her sister's mumblings as she returned the vacuum cleaner to the cupboard beneath the stairs. "I didn't realise we had any. Not serious ones anyway."

"You weren't meant to hear."

"Well, I did. Nothing wrong with my hearing." As she closed the cupboard door, the doorbell rang. Hetty, still in the hallway answered it. "Kitty, come in."

"Thanks, Het. I thought I'd pop in and see if there have been any new developments."

"Not really other than Gibson Bailey's off home and he brought me a book to read. Anyway, go and sit down: I'll put the kettle on."

Kitty stayed for less than an hour as she and Tommy needed to go shopping. After she left, Hetty and Lottie made their lunch. When everything was cleared away they put on their coats, having decided to take Albert for a walk and call in to see Debbie and Gideon en route. They arrived in St. Mary's Avenue to find Debbie painting her front door. Her husband, Gideon was out at Pentrillick House, working in the gardens.

"Lovely colour," said Hetty, admiringly, "I'm very fond of mauve."

"Me too and we've gone for this because we're going to work on a mauve and yellow colour scheme for the Pentrillick in Bloom competition next year now we know it's going ahead and we don't want the paintwork to look too new."

"Lovely idea," agreed Lottie, "Should look very nice."

"Thanks. I won't be a minute. Just finish this bit then I'll take a break before I do the door frame."

"No rush," said Hetty, "we've all the time in the world and have only come round for a gossip. Much better than phoning."

"Oh, I agree." Debbie finished the last bit of door and then placed the lid on the paint tin and her brush inside a small polythene bag. "Come on, let's go inside and out of this chilly wind."

As they stepped towards the door, Hetty noticed the curtains move in one of the upstairs windows of the neighbouring house. "I think we're being spied on," she chuckled.

Debbie tutted. "Marlene no doubt. She's been a real curtain twitcher ever since the Hamiltons arrived in the village."

"Really, I wonder why. I mean, you can't see Sea View Cottage from up here." Hetty released Albert from his lead and the little dog promptly sat down on the rug in a shaft of sunlight shining through the open door leading into the kitchen.

"No, but Angie likes to go out running and sometimes comes round this way. If Marlene's at home and spots her she nips outside and sweeps the doorstep or cleans the windows hoping to get a chance to speak to her. "

Hetty chuckled. "Probably thinks by making Angie's acquaintance she'll end up a West End star too."

"That's just what Gideon said. She also keeps popping in to see Betsy Triggs after finishing her school dinner stint, offering to help with her back garden and so forth. Betsy thinks it's hilarious as she blatantly just wants the opportunity to look over the fence into the garden of Sea View next door," Debbie glanced around the sitting room, "Shall we go in the kitchen then we can sit round the table. It's nice and sunny in there."

"So, any news?" Debbie asked once they were all seated around the table with mugs of tea.

Hetty hung Albert's lead on the back of her chair. "Not really. Gibson Bailey's off home today but that's about it. In fact Kitty popped in earlier and asked the same question as you."

"And she didn't have any news either," added Lottie.

"Oh well, I suppose Gibson going home is something. It's a shame though as he was one of your suspects, wasn't he, Het?" Debbie placed her hand over her mouth to hide a smile.

"Yes he was and he still is."

Lottie tutted. "Shame on you, Het, especially after he left you the copy of his book."

"What book's that?" Debbie asked.

"Richard Osman's."

"Oh yes. Now you come to mention it, he was reading it when I was last in the pub. Which reminds me: Serena Hamilton was in the pub the other night and was very much under the influence of alcohol." Debbie moved her chair back a few inches to avoid the sun shining in her eyes.

"Really!" Hetty placed her half empty mug down heavily on the table top. "We've not heard anything about that, so do tell us more."

"Well, apparently she was in with what's his name? You know, her brother…"

"…Drake," Hetty hastily prompted.

"That's right. Drake. Anyway, as I said the two of them were in the pub and when they first arrived she was her usual hoity-toity self, but towards closing time when she'd polished off best part of a bottle of top-of-the-range gin she got all tearful and started wailing about how Eddie was like a brother to her. She kept saying she loved him and she didn't know how she'd live without him. Tess, who told me this, said it was most embarrassing and poor Drake was mortified. Poor lad, he tried to calm her down and reminded her that up until they'd arrived in Pentrillick they'd none of them seen each other since Eddie's dad's funeral five years earlier. She wouldn't have it though and continued to make a fuss."

Lottie shook her head. "She's a right drama queen by the looks of things."

"Or," said Hetty, "could she be saying those things to cover something up?"

Debbie was correct in her assumption that her next-door neighbour Marlene was eager to make the acquaintance of either Bentley or Angie Hamilton. For Marlene despite approaching her middle years was star struck and dreamt of treading the boards in the ornate and glamorous West End theatres. In her wildest dreams she saw the rows of plush seating, the footlights, the smartly dressed musicians in the orchestra pit and the audience, each and every one applauding her talent. Such a contrast to the village hall, where rows of plastic chairs scraped on wooden floorboards and Kitty Thomas, and her next door neighbour, Gideon Elms, took it in turns to play the piano for the three nights the drama group's productions ran. For that reason Debbie would not be surprised to learn that as darkness fell later that day, the dinner lady was on the beach, feet curled beneath her on one of the wooden benches. With arms draped over the back, she watched the rear garden of Sea View Cottage, hoping that one or both of the senior Hamiltons might appear amongst the shadows and step through the garden gate onto the cliff path in order to take a stroll across the sand beneath the starlit sky. Were they to do so she'd strike up a conversation and impress them with her intelligence, wit and charm.

All was quiet as Marlene sat and patiently waited. An occasional vehicle drove along the main street and distant muffled voices and laughter drifted across the beach from the outdoor area at the back of the Crown and Anchor. The last of the gulls, replenished after a day scavenging, had departed to rest on the cliffs along the shoreline and as the tide was at its lowest, even the sound of rippling waves was little more than a murmur.

After a while the hardness of the bench caused Marlene to change her position until finally unable to get comfortable she admitted to herself that she was probably wasting her time. The church clock struck nine as she stood up in order to make her way home. But as she reached the road she changed her mind. Her husband was at work on a nightshift and both teenage children were out with their friends. Not wanting to go home to an empty house she decided instead to pop along to the Crown and Anchor for a drink. "Ange and Bent might even be there," she chuckled to herself.

With a spring in her step she walked along the pavement. When she was opposite the church she paused, for in the light of a streetlamp she saw, flopped across the bench by the bus stop, a person wearing a hooded top similar to one her son owned. Fearing it might be him having flaked out through excessive consumption of alcohol, she crossed the road to take a look. But as she neared the person she realised it was not her son, as the person in question was of a far smaller build. However, to make sure he was alright she spoke to him and after getting no response lifted his head. The hood of his top fell back and to her horror she saw a deep gash across his skull and his hair was matted with wet blood. She tried to keep calm but was shaking from head to toe. Her mind was blank; her heart was thumping; she had no idea what action to take. And then in the stillness of the night she heard the sound of a door closing nearby. She turned her head just in time to see Bentley Hamilton step onto the pavement and close the front gate of Sea View Cottage behind him.

Sensing something was wrong, Bentley stopped walking and called from across the road, "Are you alright there?"

Marlene shook her head. "No, no, I'm not. I think he's dead."

"Dead!" Bentley dashed across the road. "Have you checked for a pulse?"

"What? No, no."

He knelt down and lifted the young man's arm. "There is a pulse albeit very weak." He stood and pulled a phone from his pocket. "I assume you've not rung for help either?"

"No, um, no. I didn't think…"

Bentley dialled 999 and asked for the police and an ambulance.

"So what happened?" He asked as he returned the phone to his pocket.

"I…I don't know. I was just walking on the other side of the road and saw him here. I crossed thinking it might be my son."

"And is it?"

"No, no, it's not."

"Have you any idea who he is?"

"No. I've never seen him before in my life."

Shortly after, the emergency services arrived and the young man was taken away by ambulance. The police asked questions and Marlene told them what had happened from her point of view but knew her words were of little or no help, because she had seen no-one in the vicinity of the bus stop prior to observing the victim. Eventually, after taking their details, Marlene, eyes red from crying and make-up smudged, and Bentley, as cool as a cucumber, were allowed to go and so they walked to the Crown and Anchor. After one drink, Marlene was able to relax a little and despite her concern for the injured man, could see the funny side of the situation. For there was she, wanting to impress the Hamiltons with her confidence, capability, intelligence and charming mode of speech where in reality when faced with adversity she'd been reduced to a bumbling, dithering wreck. Knowing it was not possible to have a second attempt at a first impression, her chance to amaze was gone for ever.

# Chapter Fourteen

Inside the police station the following morning, Detective Inspector David Bray went over the known facts regarding the assault in Pentrillick at the bus stop by the church. To his dismay it was the second incident in his new home village within a month of his arrival and in both cases they had no leads other than a blood stained stone on the top of the church wall that was loose, looked to have been moved and was possibly the weapon used in the assault.

No mobile phone or any form of identification was found on the bus stop victim's person or inside the holdall bag found tucked beneath a bench which it was assumed belonged to him. Because he had no phone nor wallet it was very likely the motive for the attack was robbery and because there were no clear fingerprints on the bag other than those of the victim, it was assumed that, should he have owned a phone and wallet, then either they had been inside his pockets or the assailant had worn gloves. However, there was good some news, that being the young man had regained consciousness and his condition was not life threatening. The bad news was he was suffering from amnesia and didn't even know his name.

That same morning Norman, glad to have a reason to get out of the house, left Jackie dying her hair and drove down to the village to check that all was well in the hall having only given it a cursory glance on his last visit.

The rain drenched pavements were devoid of pedestrians and because most people were at work there was very little traffic along the street, so he was able to park outside the village hall. As he turned the key in the lock and stepped into the vestibule he instantly sensed that something was amiss. The door between the vestibule and the main function room was open; he could smell coffee yet the hall had been out of use for many months. Instinctively he crossed the wooden floor and made his way towards the kitchen - an open planned extension to the original building erected in the nineteen fifties - where a counter and roller shutters separated the kitchen from the main room of the hall. The shutters were open and so Norman could see inside. The room was tidy with no dirty mugs or evidence of use. As he opened the door and stepped inside the kitchen, he caught sight of his reflection in the chrome kettle. He paused and reached out to touch it. The metal surface was warm. Instinctively he opened the refrigerator which when not in use was always switched off and the door left part-open. Various items of food were on the shelves and a container of milk was tucked inside the door compartment. Wondering if one of the hall's committee members had placed the food items there, he left the kitchen and crossed the wooden floor to the middle of the main room. He glanced around. Everything looked as usual. Chairs were stacked alongside one wall and the curtains on the stage were closed. He left the hall and opened the door leading into a back room used for storage and by the village's drama group as a dressing room. It too looked normal. He called out. "Is anyone here?" As anticipated there was no reply but Norman thought he'd heard someone gasp. Quietly he opened a door leading onto the stage and there in the wings, huddled beneath the side-curtain, he saw two young women. Both cowered as he stepped towards them.

Seeing fear in their eyes he stooped down to their level. "I'm not going to hurt you but why are you here?"

"Who are you?" The girl spoke with a soft Yorkshire accent, "and how did you know we were here?"

"I'm the village hall's caretaker and my name is Norman. When I came in to check everything's alright I smelt coffee and when I touched the kettle I found it was warm. Then I discovered food in the fridge."

"Oh," the girl who had spoken seemed to relax. "We're not doing any harm. Honest. We just needed somewhere to stay 'til Lucy's foot gets better. She can't drive you see, so we can't get home."

Norman looked at the other girl. "What have you done to your foot, Lucy?"

"I twisted it when we were running away." She pulled back the blanket covering her legs to reveal her foot badly bruised and swollen.

"Good grief, that's needs seeing to," he looked at the uninjured girl, "What's your name, sweetheart?"

"Gemma."

"Come on then, Gemma, help me get Lucy to her feet. My van's outside and we're taking her to A & E and while I'm driving you can tell me why you're in the hall."


"Have you heard the latest?" Debbie having run up from the village was out of breath.

"No, we've not seen anyone since you the day before yesterday although Kitty rang last night to tell us about the incident at the bus stop. Nasty business that." Lottie closed the door after Debbie crossed the threshold and indicated their guest take a seat in the living room where Hetty sat by the fire doing a crossword puzzle.

"Ah, just the person. Name a breed of dog, two words, five letters and seven letters. Last letter of second word is D."

"Saint Bernard," Debbie removed her jacket and hung it on the back of the nearest dining chair.

Hetty tutted. "Of course, silly me." She filled in the empty spaces.

"You got that pretty quick," Lottie was impressed.

"That's because when I was a girl I craved a Saint Bernard. Must have been mad as we lived in a modest house in a town with a small back garden. No wonder Mum and Dad both said no."

"You could have one now though," reasoned Lottie, "your garden here is a good size and there are loads of places to walk."

Debbie sat down. "I could but the thought lost its appeal more years ago than I care to remember."

"So, what's the latest news?" Hetty dropped the magazine on the floor and removed her spectacles. "Has the young man who was attacked at the bus stop got his memory back?"

"I don't know but there might be a connection between him and my news. You see, Jackie and Norman have guests. Two girls from Sheffield who are, or should I were, fans of Eddie Madigan."

"Really?"

Lottie raised her hand. "Don't say any more for a minute or two, Debbie. This sounds like a coffee and cake moment. I'll put the kettle on." She hastily bustled from the room.

When all were seated with mugs of steaming coffee, Debbie began to relay her news. "Well, I've just seen Tess who as you know works with Jackie at the pub and she told me in great detail about the girls. As I said earlier, they're big fans of poor Eddie and the band he used to play with and so when they saw on social media that he'd

102

come down here to Cornwall they asked around to find out whereabouts and then did the same after telling family and friends they were off to Cornwall for a holiday before the new academic year starts. They're students, you see."

"But surely they should be getting ready to go back by now," reasoned Lottie, "I know Vicki and Kate are off this weekend."

"Yes, but they've told the folks back home that they're perfectly well but have both tested positive for Covid and so have to self-isolate for ten days."

"They shouldn't be with Norman and Jackie then." Hetty was horrified.

"Yes, but it's not true. They made it up in order to stay longer because they didn't want to worry their families."

"But why?" Hetty was confused.

"Because they didn't want to worry their parents by saying Lucy had injured her foot, I suppose."

"Insured her foot?" Hetty queried, "What's she done to it?"

"I'll come to that in a minute. Now where was I? Oh yes, right, well as you'll already have gathered one of the girls is called Lucy. The other one is Gemma. Lucy has a van which when they first got here they used to sleep in rather than fork out for bed and breakfast accommodation or whatever. And then Lucy badly sprained her foot and was unable to walk, so they broke into the village hall and stayed there knowing they'd be safe because the notice on the board outside says there are no scheduled events until bingo starts again on September the twenty-first."

"And Norman found them," pre-empted Lottie.

"Precisely. He found them yesterday morning when he went to make sure everything was alright."

"How did they get into the hall?" Hetty asked, "I mean, that front door is really solid."

Debbie nodded. "An ill-fitting window in the ladies toilet. Apparently the catch is broken so it only needs a good tug to open it."

"But those windows are tiny," gasped Lottie.

"Well, perhaps the girls are tiny too," reasoned Debbie, "anyway I should imagine only Gemma went in through the window. I mean, Lucy couldn't have done it because of her foot, could she? So Gemma must have let her in through the back door which if you remember has no lock, just a series of bolts. Something like that. Anyway, once inside the girls made themselves at home with their sleeping bags and slept in the wings on the stage and that's where Norman found them huddled together and as scared as church mice."

Hetty smiled. "I thought church mice were either poor or quiet, I've never heard of them being scared."

"Don't be pernickety, Het, you know what I mean."

"So what have they done for food and so forth?" Lottie asked, "And how long have they been there?"

Debbie shrugged her shoulders. "I don't know how long they've been there but they had food in the fridge so I suppose Gemma popped out and bought stuff from the shop when necessary. As for anything else, if you think about it they'd have everything they'd need in the hall for a short time anyway. Running water, use of the kitchen, toilets and so forth."

"Just as well the electricity is never switched off," said Hetty.

Lottie shuddered. "I don't think I'd like to camp out in the hall. Not with the stern faces of the village's forefathers looking down from those large picture frames."

"Probably why they chose to sleep in the wings on stage," chuckled Hetty.

Debbie nodded. "I agree. And anyway, they're alright now because as I've already said they're staying with

Norman and Jackie in their spare room 'til Lucy's foot's better and she can drive home."

"That's good and I should imagine they'll enjoy each other's company," said Hetty. "I know the lockdowns got Norman down and no doubt Jackie too, especially when the pub was shut for weeks on end."

"So did they ever get to see young Eddie before he...?" Lottie found herself unable to complete her question.

Debbie smiled. "Yes but only from a distance, which reminds me, that's why there might be a connection between this and the chap in hospital. The girls spying on Eddie, that is. You see, on the night he disappeared they were watching his caravan. Something they had done for several days before I might add. Anyway, they got there as usual around half past six and hid in their usual place amongst the shrubs. They could see someone in the caravan and assumed it was Eddie. A few minutes later said person came out and ran across the field towards the pub and car park. The girls reasoned it was Eddie gone for a shower or something like that. However, while they waited for him to come back another person arrived at the caravan carrying a guitar and cans of beer. He knocked on the door and when no-one answered, he sat down on the steps. After a few minutes the person on the steps went inside the caravan and the girls heard him call out Eddie's name. Shortly after he came back out, minus guitar and beer, and went towards the pub. Still no sign of the first person but eventually the second person came back, went inside the caravan and came back out with his guitar and cans of beer. He then walked back across the pub field. They waited another half hour but nothing else happened and so went back to Lucy's van and then drove to Penzance to get a pizza."

"Well, the second person was obviously young Dee from next door," said Hetty, "because as I've already told you I saw him on his way home looking really fed up because he hadn't met up with Eddie as planned."

"That's just what I thought," said Debbie, "What's more, it must have been either Lucy or Gemma that Marlene saw when she was walking by the pub field who we all thought could have been Eddie's erstwhile girlfriend, Willow."

"Yes, of course," said Hetty. "At least that's answered that question."

Lottie agreed. "The question now though is, who was the first person the girls saw on the field? The one who left the caravan before Dee arrived and didn't come back."

Hetty took a slice of chocolate cake from the tray. "Can the girls describe that person do you know, Debbie? The first, I mean, because we know the second was Dee."

"Not really because he or she wore dark clothes and a hooded top with the hood up."

"And you think it might be the bloke in hospital," gasped Hetty.

"Yes."

"Have they told the police?" Lottie asked.

"Yes. Norman rang them as soon as the girls told their story."

"Good old Norman."

"And there's more," said Debbie, "Apparently they went back again the following night not knowing that Eddie was missing of course and watched the caravan as usual. While there a person wearing dark clothes and a hooded top crept across the field constantly looking over their shoulder. When they got to the caravan they crept inside and the girls could see a torch light flashing around the walls. Both sensed something was wrong and so decided to leave. As they moved away from their hiding place, they heard the caravan door fling open and heard someone shout. The girls were scared stiff and convinced that whoever he was, was going to chase after them. It was

106

as they ran across the field that Lucy fell, tripped or whatever and twisted her ankle. Meanwhile a car pulled up outside the pub and several people got out. The girls were able to relax then and went back to Lucy's van knowing that whoever had been in the caravan wouldn't give chase if there were people around. The next morning Lucy's ankle was badly swollen and she could hardly walk. They couldn't get to A & E because Gemma doesn't drive and that's when they decided to see if they could get into the village hall and hide until Lucy's ankle went down."

"Hmm. I think," said Hetty, "it's time we called on Norman and Jackie."

Lottie frowned. "But we can't just turn up out the blue and expect to interrogate the poor girls."

"You're right, we can't. We need a plan. Any suggestions?"

"How about we pretend we want to hire the hall for something or other," said Debbie, "I'm sure we must be able to think of something plausible."

"Good thinking," agreed Hetty, "and then we can cancel the booking for whatever we've come up with saying we've changed our minds."

Lottie tutted. "I think you two are overlooking something. That being Norman is just the caretaker and has nothing to do with bookings and so forth."

"Damn. I'd forgotten that." Hetty scratched her head.

Lottie took a slice of cake from the plate and held it up. "How about one of us makes a cake and then we take it to Cobblestone Close and say we've heard about the girl's ordeal and we've made something to cheer them up. That way no lies and no deceit."

"Of course, that's a brilliant idea, Lottie. Calling on the sick is a very neighbourly thing to do. Even if we do have an ulterior motive."

107

"As well as a cake we can take a box of chocolates," said Debbie, "we still have loads unopened from Christmas and Gideon seldom eats them. He's more of a pickles man."

"They're not out of date, are they?" Lottie asked.

"No, I checked the other day and they're fine for a few weeks yet."

"That's solved then," said Hetty, "Lottie, you made a Victoria sandwich this morning. If you get some jam in it and ice the top, we can take that."

"Ideal. I'll do feather icing right now so it has time to dry."

Hetty clapped her hands with glee. "And so we all have something to offer, I suggest we take a bunch of flowers too. We've some lovely chrysanths in the back garden."

"A bit like the three kings," chuckled Debbie.

Lottie placed the empty plates and mugs on a tray. "Hmm, except that as well as being royal, the three kings were reputed to be wise."

# Chapter Fifteen

The ladies arrived at Cobblestone Close mid-afternoon each bearing a gift. Norman answered the door. The smile that swept across his face indicated he was not at all surprised to see them.

"We've heard all about the terrible ordeal and suffering the two young ladies taking refuge here with you and Jackie have had to endure and come here today to offer them our deepest, deepest sympathy," Hetty held up a bunch of yellow chrysanthemums.

"Oh, don't overdo it, Het," hissed Lottie.

Grinning, Norman opened the door wide. "Come in, ladies and we'll get the kettle on."

Debbie was first over the threshold closely followed by Hetty and then Lottie. Once inside they were led by Norman into the sitting room where the two girls were seated on a sofa. Jackie was also home, sitting cross-legged on the floor painting her nails. Against the arm of the sofa where Lucy sat, leaned a pair of crutches.

"Girls you have visitors," Norman introduced all to each other and the overwhelmed girls thanked the well-wishers for their gifts.

Gemma rose from the couch and sat on down the floor to make room for the ladies. Debbie and Hetty thanked her and sat down beside Lucy whose injured foot rested on a cushioned stool. Lottie took a seat in an armchair by the window as Norman left for the kitchen with the flowers and cake.

"How's your foot, Lucy?" Lottie asked.

"Much better already, thank you. Norman thought it might be broken but an x-ray showed it's just a bad sprain so hopefully I'll be able to put my weight on it soon."

"That's good and what a beautiful room to convalesce in," enthused Lottie, "So bright and airy."

"It is," agreed Debbie, "and what a lovely view, you can see right down the Close as far as the lane."

Jackie chuckled, "Yes, ideal for keeping an eye on the neighbours."

"I take it that van parked outside belongs to one of you girls," Hetty pointed towards the window.

"Yes, it's mine," said Lucy, "Norman very kindly went down to the village this morning to get it for me and to collect our belongings from the hall. I was anxious about it you see. I'd left it parked along the main street and was worried it might be in somebody's way."

"You also thought it might not start," said Gemma, "after all it's often temperamental and had not been driven for some time."

Debbie noticed Gemma's eyes kept darting towards the box of chocolates. "Feel free to open them, girls. After all they are for you."

"Thank you," Gemma removed the cellophane, took one for herself, offered the box to Lucy and then passed it around to everyone else. As she sat back down, Norman entered the room with mugs of tea on a tray along with a vase containing the chrysanthemums and slices of the Victoria sandwich on a plate. Jackie leapt forwards and cleared a space on the coffee table for the tray. She then placed the chrysanthemums on the window sill.

"So can either of you remember anything about the person you saw running across the pub field on the night Eddie disappeared and do you think he was the same person who you saw go into the caravan the following night?" Hetty considered enough small talk had been made and it was time to get down to business.

110

"Well to be honest on the first evening we thought it was Eddie himself crossing the field going for a shower or something like that as he had done on other days when he got back from work. Of course we now know it wasn't. As for the following night, we're pretty certain the figure we saw was the same person as the first night but couldn't say one hundred percent. What do you think, Gemma?"

"I agree with you. They certainly wore similar clothes."

"In that case, the person in question must be the same height and build as Eddie for you to have thought it might be him on the first night." Lottie nodded her thanks as Jackie handed her a mug of tea.

"Definitely. Having said that it's not possible to be really sure because there was nothing to judge his height by and we were kneeling down too, which didn't help."

"So we're looking for someone who is slimish and roughly five foot nine tall," calculated Debbie.

"Eddie was five foot seven and a half inches," smiled Lucy, "I remember reading that on the band's Facebook page. He was the shortest of the four and insisted the half inch was included."

"So he could even have been a she."

"Absolutely. I'm five foot seven when I can stand up straight on both legs." Lucy cast a scornful look at her foot.

"Could the person you saw have been Eddie's erstwhile girlfriend?" Debbie asked.

"What Willow?" Gemma was surprised by the question, "I suppose it could have been but I'm sure it wasn't. Willow has long blonde hair, but then we've no idea what the hair of the person we saw was like because it was hidden beneath the hood. I'm sure it wasn't Willow though. She's dainty and this person had a clumpy walk."

"Do you know Willow then?" Lottie asked.

The girls looked at each other and then shrugged their shoulders. "We know of her," said Gemma, "because she

111

was with Eddie for a year or so, and although we've seen her from time to time, we've never been anywhere near close enough to get chatting."

"I see," said Debbie, "Well, never mind, it was just a thought and I mentioned it because according to posts on social media she appears to be missing."

"Not surprised," said Gemma, "I should imagine she took the split with Eddie pretty badly and now for him to be, well, you know...gone, she'd just want to be alone. I know I would if I were in her shoes."

Debbie, wishing she had not mentioned the ex-girlfriend, nodded her acknowledgement.

"Anyway, I don't think it was a female," said Hetty. "My money's on it being the bloke in hospital and the reason he was at the bus stop yesterday was because he was trying to leave the village. Meaning he's not a local."

Lottie shook her head. "No, I have to disagree, Het. Because if he were one and the same he'd have scarpered after whatever happened to Eddie and not hung around until yesterday. What's more if it is him, why did someone bash him over the head?"

"Perhaps I should ask Marlene if the bloke she found was around five foot seven," suggested Debbie, "after all she only lives next door to me and apart from Bentley Hamilton she's the only one in the village who has actually seen him."

"Can't really see the point though," reasoned Lottie, "I mean the police will do all that."

"Yes, I suppose so."

Gemma took another chocolate and washed it down with tea. "I wish we could help and tell you more but there's nothing else to add and we've talked about it loads haven't we, Lucy, but all we can really say is what we told the police. That being, whoever it was wore jeans and a dark hoodie. Couldn't even say whether it was black, navy or whatever."

"Was it plain or did it have a name plastered across the back?" Debbie asked.

"We're pretty sure it was plain on the back because no image springs to mind. There might have been a name or something on the front though, but if there was we didn't see it."

Lucy nodded her head. "That's right and with hindsight I wish we'd been more observant."

Hetty sighed. "Oh dear. So the description you've given fits just about anyone."

"Sadly yes." Lucy moved her foot on the stool to get more comfortable.

"How about the voice," said Debbie, "Tess told me that on the second night whoever it was shouted at you. What did he or she say and was the voice deep like a bloke or high-pitched?"

Gemma looked at Lucy and pulled a face. "That's a tricky one, isn't it, Lucy? I mean it wasn't really deep or high pitched but sort of in-between."

"That's right and he only said 'Oy' anyway so not really much to go on."

Debbie's shoulders slumped. "Oh well, there's nothing else I can think of to ask."

Having finished her tea, Gemma took a slice of Lottie's Victoria sandwich. "I'm really sorry we can't help much and wish we could because we both hate the thought of Ed's death being unsolved."

"We do," agreed Lucy, "and with hindsight I wish we'd taken pictures on our phones. The thought never crossed our minds though but I suppose in reality there wouldn't really have been enough time anyway."

"And it was also quite dull and so any pictures we might have taken wouldn't have shown any more detail than we remember."

"Never mind, but if you do think of anything else do let us know," said Lottie.

Lucy smiled. "That's exactly what the nice policeman said."

"What was the name of the police officer who questioned you?" Hetty asked.

Gemma frowned. "There were two of them. A man and a woman. The woman was Jane something or other but I can't remember the bloke's name."

"It was your next door neighbour, Het," said Norman.

"David Bray. Excellent." Hetty gleefully rubbed her hands together.

"Hoping to wangle a bit of information out of him, are you?" laughed Norman.

"As if I would."

Lottie nodded her head. "She would if she could."

Hetty stood, "I think we've taken up enough of your time and so we'll make a move."

The girls again thanked the ladies for their gifts and said it was nice to have met them.

Jackie chatted as she showed the ladies to the door. "The two girls from the pasty shop were in the pub last night talking to Sally and Robert Oliver. I introduced them because they asked about bowling at Pentrillick House. They fancy taking up a sport, you see, but don't want anything too strenuous as they're on their feet all day in the shop. I mention it because Sally told them that you being near neighbours played from time to time so you might want to set up a match."

"That would be lovely," said Lottie, "I'll tell them we're keen next time we're in the pasty shop."

"So will their chaps play too?" Debbie asked.

"I don't expect so. Jude has joined the pub's pool team and apparently every Tuesday and Thursday Dennis goes kick-boxing somewhere in Penzance. That's why the girls wanted a hobby too."

After Jackie had waved them goodbye and closed the door, Hetty let out a deep breath. "Did you hear that?

Kick-boxing. Dennis has taken up kick-boxing. Well we know different, don't we, ladies?"

"We certainly do," said Lottie, "the question now is, what are we going to do about it?"

"Are you doing anything special on Thursday evening, Debbie?" Hetty asked.

"No, not as far as I know."

"Good, because I suggest on Thursday night, we are all ready and waiting at our place and follow Dennis to Penzance to see what he's really up to? We'll ask Kitty along too."

"But why?" Lottie asked.

"Because we need to establish whether the woman he was with when Debbie and Gideon saw them is just an acquaintance he happened to bump into or if it's something more. If he meets her again then it's definitely something more and as we've agreed before, if Eddie found out and threatened to tell Dolly, then Dennis Sharpe has a strong motive for murder."

# Chapter Sixteen

Following the interview with the two girls from Sheffield, the police conducted a search in the village of the area around the bus stop where the unidentified attack victim was found, hoping to find a connection between him and the man seen running from Eddie Madigan's caravan. To their dismay, the search was unproductive and so the young man's identity remained unknown. However, later that same day, Vicki and Kate, having the day off work and looking forward to shopping in Truro, were sitting on the bench where the young man was found. As they waited for a bus they heard a sound they recognised as indication a phone battery was in the throes of dying. The sound came from somewhere behind. Curious, they both stood and tried to establish the sound's whereabouts. Vicki thought it came from inside the churchyard but Kate was adamant it was nearer and most likely the church's stone wall. After poking her fingers in several crevices, Kate pulled out a mobile phone; tucked behind it, was a wallet. In the wallet was a driving licence and its photograph depicted a young man. His name was Lewis Peters. Behind the licence was a card with his address - 31a, Gold Street, Leeds. Wondering if the young man might be the unidentified person in hospital, Kate promptly took out her phone and rang the police.

After establishing a resounding likeness between the driving licence photograph and the patient in hospital, the police assumed they were one and the same. They then contacted the force in the Leeds area and requested their assistance with the case. Two officers were sent to the address found in the wallet where they established that Lewis Peters lived alone. Neighbours were questioned but knew nothing of his movements except for one person who was able to tell them that Lewis worked as a mechanic at a garage. A visit to the garage followed, but all the officers were able to glean was that Lewis had taken the week off work and the garage's proprietor had no idea of his plans. However, on the day of Lewis Peter's accident, the police in Cornwall had found inside his pocket, train and bus tickets, but not knowing his identity at that time they had been of little use. Now, due to the latest discovery it was assumed Lewis had travelled down from Leeds by rail and taken a bus from Penzance to Pentrillick. A chat with the driver of the eight-fifteen bus recalled dropping off a young man wearing a hooded top at the bus stop in Pentrillick but the only details he could recall were that the young man carried a holdall, was polite, travelled alone and there was no-one at the stop when he alighted. With the evidence gathered it was obvious to all concerned that if Lewis Peters was the man in hospital then he was not in the village when Eddie Madigan met his death.

It was misty when the sisters arose on Thursday but by mid-morning the sun was out, and because they were eager for the day to pass as quickly as possible, they went outside after breakfast to clean the greenhouse ready to house tender plants for the long winter months. Tomato plants were still growing inside but on each there was only a little unripe fruit left so they gathered what there was with every intention of making green tomato chutney. Cleaning the greenhouse was a chore neither relished and so once the staging and everything else stored inside was removed they tossed a coin to establish who should clean what. Consequently, Hetty washed down the outside glass and Lottie scrubbed the inside. When the job was finished and the glass gleamed in the sunlight the sisters returned indoors for a coffee break, congratulating themselves on a job well done.

While Lottie made the coffee, Hetty went into the sitting room and switched on the News channel hoping for an update on Eddie's case, for they knew through Bill and Sandra that the twins had found a mobile phone and wallet, and it was assumed both belonged to the mystery man in hospital. Should that prove correct, then it was unlikely the mystery man was linked in any way to Eddie's death. However, people could only surmise, for at that point the police had not released any information on the subject. To Hetty's dismay the news made no reference to Eddie and much of its content they had heard at breakfast time. But as Lottie entered the room with the coffee, *Breaking News*, flashed across the screen announcing the death of opera singer, Leonardo Riccioni who had died earlier that day aged eighty seven. Hetty's mouth gaped open in surprise. "But…what…I mean…"

"You told me you'd made the name up."

"That's because I did."

"Well clearly not." Lottie handed her sister a mug of coffee and then sat down.

"But that's ridiculous. I mean, what a coincidence that there really is, or should I say was, an opera singer of that name."

Lottie shook her head. "You should have Googled the name, Het, to check it out, especially after poor Gibson Bailey claimed to know of him."

Hetty frowned. "Why is Gibson Bailey poor?"

"Because you unjustly suspected he might have played a part in Eddie's death."

"He still might have."

"No way, Het, and it's not likely to be the chap in hospital either because everyone reckons he wasn't even here and had only just arrived when he was attacked."

"True, I suppose. Which brings in yet another conundrum: why was he attacked at the bus stop and left for dead, and why, if the phone and wallet are his, did someone stuff them in the church wall?"

"No idea, but going back to Eddie's death, to suggest it was Gibson who pushed him from the cliff path is silly because according to the girls we're looking for someone who is slimish and around five foot seven. Gibson is neither slim nor that height. He's got to be a good six foot tall and I very much doubt he owns a hooded top."

"Okay. So it looks like I made a mistake. Anyway, after all that hard work how about fish and chips for lunch?" Wanting to avoid digging herself into a hole, Hetty knew her best option was to change the subject.

"Sounds perfect and as I'm feeling peckish, let's go down now."

"Good idea and we'll take Albert so he can stretch his legs."

At the bottom of Long Lane they crossed the road and stepped onto the pavement outside the Crown and Anchor. As they turned towards the main part of the village they heard a voice call from behind. It was Sandra, Lottie's daughter-in-law on her way back from her shift in the care home for the elderly where she worked part-time.

"Glad to have caught you," puffed Sandra, "save me ringing. I was going to ask you round for lunch tomorrow, you see. Nothing too special but just a little get together before the girls go back off to uni on Sunday. I know it's short notice but we only decided over breakfast this morning. Do hope you can make it. Zac and Emma will be there too."

"Sounds lovely," said Lottie, "We'll be there won't we, Het?"

119

"Absolutely, so what time shall we call?"

"Whenever you're ready. We'll probably eat around half-oneish and then have nibbles in the evening. I thought we could make a day of it. You know, a bit like Christmas, seeing as Christmas was sort of cancelled last year."

Sandra walked along the pavement with the sisters chatting of the recent happenings in the village.

"Did you know they've confirmed the name of the poor lad in hospital?" Feeling warm, Sandra unzipped her jacket.

"No, we didn't," said Lottie, "so does that mean the wallet and phone the twins found definitely belong to him?"

"Yes. Apparently the lad had a good day yesterday and when a police officer showed him the driving licence he recognised it and said it was his."

"That's wonderful. So who is he?" Hetty asked, "I know you mentioned a name when the items were found but it went in one ear and out the other."

"He's Lewis Peters and he's from Leeds. 31a, Gold Street to be exact. He came down by train and then caught a bus to Pentrillick. The police reckon he was attacked within minutes of getting here."

Hetty stopped walking as Albert sniffed around the base of a lamppost. "That's one thing settled then. I mean, it definitely couldn't have been him the girls saw on the pub field because he wasn't even here then."

Lottie slowed her pace to allow her sister to catch up. "So, I wonder, why was he here?"

"Came down for a holiday I suppose," reasoned Hetty, "I mean people do, don't they?"

"Yes, but not usually alone."

"True, and if he was down for a holiday, I wonder where he was going to stay." Hetty fell back in step with her sister and niece.

"The pub perhaps or even the Pentrillick Hotel," suggested Sandra, "I'm sure the police will ask around now they know his name. Or he might even remember himself."

By the fish and chip shop the sisters stopped. "This is as far as we go, Sandra," said Lottie, "we're having fish and chips for lunch to replace the calories burned cleaning the greenhouse."

"Very nice too."

Inside the fish and chip shop the Haddocks were busy serving four young men who were strangers to the sisters. When their turn came they were served by Matilda.

"Nice to see you ladies. What can I get you?"

"Cod and chips twice, please." Lottie took her purse from her pocket.

"To take away?"

"Yes, please."

"Anymore news about the chap who was attacked?" Matilda asked, "The police were giving the area a real going over yesterday morning and someone said something about a wallet and phone being found."

"Actually, yes," said Hetty, always happy to pass on information. "His wallet and driving licence have been found and it was Lottie's granddaughters who found them. It's assumed he'd come down for a holiday," she paused. "Now let me get this right. His name is Lewis Peters and he lives in Leeds at 31a, Gold Street."

The colour drained from Matilda's face; she dropped the fish scoop and Garfield flung his arms around her lest she fall in a faint.

"What did I say wrong?" Hetty's voice shook.

"Not your fault, love," said Garfield, leading his wife to a chair, "but Matilda's son is called Lewis Peters and he lives at 31a, Gold Street in Leeds."

# Chapter Seventeen

Unsure of the time Dennis might leave for his supposed kick-boxing club, Debbie and Kitty arrived at Primrose Cottage at five o'clock in order that they all be ready to leave the minute they saw either the window cleaning van or one of the cars the occupants of Fuchsia Cottage owned, drive by. Debbie who had volunteered to take her car, had parked it facing the open gates when she'd arrived, ready for them to make a quick getaway. Meanwhile, to make sure Dennis didn't slip by unnoticed, they took it in turns to sit at the table by the window and watch the lane. At seven o'clock, Kitty heard an engine start up. She sprang from the chair. "That has to be him and he's taking the van. I recognise the sound of the engine."

The ladies already wearing jackets, grabbed their handbags and made for the door just as Dennis drove by.

"Quick, we don't want to lose him." Hetty locked the front door and dropped the key into her pocket.

"No need to panic," said Debbie, "we know which way he's going."

There was no sign of the van as they reached the junction at the bottom of Long Lane but a little further on as they approached Vince's Garage they spotted it turning onto the main road. Keeping well back they followed the van to Penzance where it drove through the town and then eventually pulled up in Wisteria Avenue opposite a row of large detached houses. Rather than drive past, Debbie pulled into a space at the side of the road beneath a silver birch tree where they watched Dennis leave his vehicle and approach a house through a small but beautifully manicured front garden. At the top of steps on either side of the front door, exotic grasses in large ceramic planters, swayed in the evening breeze. As soon as Dennis knocked, the door was opened and he went inside.

"Now what?" Lottie asked, "I mean, he could be in there for ages."

"Might even be the place where they do kick-boxing," reasoned Kitty, "after all, we didn't see who answered the door."

Hetty shook her head. "Maybe, but my money's on it being the home of Dennis's fancy-woman."

"I agree," said Debbie, "and if it is her, her place must be worth a pretty penny. I bet it's enormous inside and no doubt there's a gorgeous garden out the back."

"Looks like she's a woman with money then," said Hetty. "Either that or she has a rich husband who is away."

Five minutes later the door opened and Dennis appeared with a woman by his side.

Debbie gasped. "Oh yes, that's her. She's the one Gideon and I saw him with."

"Now what?" Kitty ducked, as did the others as the couple walked by on the opposite side of the road.

"Shall we follow them?" Debbie was itching to see where they went.

"I'm game if you all are," Hetty unfastened her seat belt.

Neither Lottie nor Kitty replied for they had already opened their car doors.

"To make ourselves look less conspicuous, I suggest we split up and avoid walking beneath the streetlamps." Hetty took Kitty's arm. "You walk on this side with me, Kitty and you other two can walk on the other side."

"But what if they turn round and see us?" Lottie asked, "*She* won't recognise us but Dennis knows you and me by sight and Kitty's his landlady."

"Good point. Do any of you have sunglasses with you?"

"I do," said Debbie, "but there's no way I'm wearing them when it's getting dark. I'd look daft."

"How about masks then?" Hetty was running short of ideas.

The ladies acknowledged they always carried masks in their handbags and although it wasn't necessary when out in the fresh air with very few people around, they agreed to put them on. Once disguises were in place they walked briskly to shorten the gap between themselves and the couple they were in pursuit of.

After a while the couple turned into a pedestrianised street.

"Oh dear. I've a sneaky feeling they're going to the cinema," whispered Debbie, as they briefly grouped back together in a shop doorway.

"You could well be right," Kitty agreed, "So do we still follow them?"

The consensus to continue was unanimous but in case Dennis and the unknown woman should turn round, the ladies walked individually, taking it in turns to look in shop windows. Outside the cinema the couple stopped and then went inside.

"Right. What now?" groaned Hetty, "Do we wait 'til they come out or go in and watch a film?"

"I'd rather watch a film than stand out here looking like a lemon for a couple of hours," confessed Lottie.

The others agreed.

"There's just one problem," said Debbie, "the cinema has four screens so we'll not know which film they've gone to see."

"Not a problem," declared Kitty, "there are four of us so we'll split up and take one each."

Lottie took a seat on the back row for her screening, for they had all agreed the back would be the best place to keep a look-out for Dennis and his friend. However, after a good look round she decided they were not present and as the film she had been allocated seemed rather boring, and she was tired after a busy morning cleaning the greenhouse, she fell asleep within the first thirty minutes.

Things were much the same for Kitty. The couple were nowhere to be seen but as the film was to her liking she was able to enjoy it without interruptions. It was Debbie who found herself in the presence of Dennis and his friend. She spotted them as soon as she entered the auditorium. They were seated on the back row at the opposite end to herself. Not wanting to be seen, she quickly sat down. To disguise her appearance, she pulled her hair back into a ponytail, put on her reading glasses and adjusted her mask to cover as much of her face as possible. When the lights came on during the intermission, she took out her phone, kept her head bowed low and pretended to scroll down the screen while keeping a watchful eye. But apart from buying ice creams, there was nothing of any consequence to report.

At the fourth screening, Hetty, none too keen on the film passed the time eating popcorn. When the lights went on during the intermission, she heard a voice call her name. "Miss Tonkins, we meet again." Hetty looked up. Seated on the row in front of her towards the aisle sat recently-retired, Detective Inspector Fox. "Oh, Detective Inspector, how lovely to see you," Hetty hoped her statement sounded convincing.

"Likewise. Mind if I join you? I feel a bit of a twit on my own." Before she had time to answer he had climbed over the seating and was sitting beside her. "I must say I wouldn't have put you down for liking this genre of film. I would have thought Miss Marple or Midsomer Murders more to your liking."

As she thought how best to reply she saw a twinkle in his eyes. "You're pulling my leg."

"Yes, I am. Sorry." He glanced at the empty seat on Hetty's left, "Your sister not with you?"

"No, that is to say, yes, but she's watching a different film."

"Very wise of her. I wish I'd done the same."

Not wishing to pursue the subject of Lottie being in the same building, Hetty asked the retired DI if he was serious about moving to Pentrillick.

"Absolutely, I think it's a smashing spot. I've already sold my place in Hayle and my stuff's in storage. I'm currently in digs here in Penzance and so now just need to find the right place. It's not looking too good though as a lot of people are moving to the country from towns and cities hoping they'll be able to continue to work from home. Which of course means there's not a great deal on the market and when something does come up it's snapped up in minutes."

"So, I've heard. Still, fingers crossed, eh and if you've sold your place you're in a very good position to buy, Inspector."

"I am and please call me Paul, after all I am retired now."

"Oh, but that doesn't sound right. A bit like calling an old schoolmaster by his Christian name. Not of course that you're old enough to be an old schoolmaster of mine. In fact you must be several years my junior."

"I'm fifty-nine."

"I see, so just a couple of years my junior then."

"Plus eight," chuckled Paul, "I'm ten years your junior."

Hetty's jaw dropped, "How do you know that?"

"Your date of birth cropped up on one of your many police visits. The date registered with me, you see, because you and your sister have the same birthday as me. With ten years in between, I might add. You two being born in 1952 and me in 1962."

"Well, I never. So you'll be sixty in February."

"Yes, and you and your sister will be…"

"Don't say it," interrupted Hetty, "It's a subject Lottie and I have agreed to avoid."

"What a shame. We could have had a joint birthday party. Me celebrating my sixtieth and you four score years and ten."

For once in her life, Hetty was lost for words.

Later as the film credits rolled, Hetty and the retired inspector made their way towards the foyer where Hetty hoped he might bid her farewell before he spotted not just her sister, but Debbie and Kitty also. Her hopes did not come to fruition, for the three ladies, their films having finished earlier, had already bumped into each other and so arrived together. The retired DI raised his eyebrows. "You're all here, I see."

On seeing him, Debbie gasped, "Oh, Detective Inspector Fox, how nice to see you," she lied, "and yes, we couldn't agree which film to watch so split up and went our separate ways."

The retired detective inspector laughed as he tried to fathom out if there was an ulterior motive for the ladies' trip to the cinema. At that moment Dennis and his female friend entered the foyer. The ladies not wishing to be seen, turned their heads until the couple were out of sight.

"Well," said Paul, "it looks as though Caroline has found herself a toy boy. Good for her."

"Caroline? Who is Caroline?" Hetty asked on seeing the coast was clear.

"Caroline Bates. Ex-wife of Ambrose Bates the multi-millionaire."

The retired DI smiled on seeing four blank expressions. "Ambrose and Caroline divorced earlier this year when he found himself a woman half Caroline's age. She came out of the marriage with a favourable settlement and bought herself a place here in Penzance where she's able to enjoy a very healthy bank balance. She's a Cornish lass, and after enjoying the high-life has returned to her roots."

"Would that be the blonde woman I spotted watching the same film as me?" Debbie asked, trying to be subtle. "A blonde, dressed in blue carrying a Gucci handbag and wearing matching shoes. Early to mid-fifties, I'd say. Very pretty and beautifully made up."

"You are observant, but yes, that'd be her. Anyway, I must take my leave now as I have a busy day house hunting tomorrow. Well, that is to say I have one place to look at but I don't hold out much hope."

"Oh, I see, well, yes, goodbye then, Paul," said Hetty, "and I hope you find somewhere suitable soon."

"Paul," hissed Debbie, as Paul Fox left the building, "since when have you and he been on first name terms?"

Hetty felt her cheeks redden. "Since I saw him inside the cinema. I didn't realise 'til the lights went on that he was sitting on the row in front of me. He was all alone and asked if he could join me. That's when he said to call him Paul. I mean, Detective Inspector is a bit of a mouthful."

"Yes, but he's an ex-copper," spluttered Debbie.

"I disagree, Debbie, and say, good for you, Het. I mean, it might be useful to have him as an acquaintance." Lottie clearly approved of her sister's actions.

Kitty nodded in agreement. "Meanwhile, we must meet tomorrow to discuss tonight's discovery further, because this changes everything. If Dennis has caught himself a *wealthy* woman he'd have no need of any cash tied up in the pasty shop and so he wouldn't have had a motive to kill poor Eddie, had Eddie threatened to tell Dolly about this Caroline woman."

Debbie gasped. "Good point, Kitty. In fact Dennis would most likely have been relieved, because it'd save him the unpleasant task of doing it."

Lottie nodded. "I agree that we need to look into it but we can't meet tomorrow because Hetty and I are off to the Old Bakehouse for the day for a get together before the twins go back to uni."

"In that case I suggest we meet on Saturday around elevenish," said Kitty, "the usual venue, Primrose Cottage."

Everyone agreed.

# Chapter Eighteen

Sitting around the table at the twins' farewell lunch inside the Old Bakehouse, the family discussed the recent happenings in the village. Mainly they focussed on the death of Eddie Madigan, but the arrival of Gemma and Lucy, and more recently, the young man attacked at the bus stop being the son of Matilda Haddock and the twins finding his wallet and phone, also took up a fair amount of time. However because, while walking down Long Lane on their way to meet the family, Hetty and Lottie had agreed to keep quiet about their trip to the cinema, Dennis Sharpe's new 'friend' did not get a mention.

"Does anyone know how Matilda's lad is?" Lottie asked, "The last we heard was he had amnesia and didn't know his name until he was shown his driving licence."

"He's doing alright," said Zac, "The Haddocks came in the pub around half-nine last night after they'd been to visit him in hospital, along with the police wanting to question him, I might add. Garfield said that seeing his mum had jogged his memory a little and it's slowly starting to come back. Apparently he was here to pay them a surprise visit. He vaguely remembers the train journey now and getting on the bus but sadly nothing after that."

"Oh, that's so sweet," sighed Lottie, "Planning to surprise them, I mean. It's the sort of thing we'd have done when we were young, isn't it, Het?"

"Yes and I still like surprising people today."

"But it doesn't make sense," said Sandra, "The assault, that is. I mean, why would anyone attack someone who'd only just arrived? He'd have been a stranger to anyone other than the Haddocks."

"Perhaps he was followed here by someone who had something against him," suggested Kate.

"Probably even followed him down here all the way from Leeds," added Vicki.

Bill frowned. "But if that's the case, why wait until they got here to hit him?"

"Because this was the first place he could get near him that was quiet," reasoned Vicki, "I mean, he could hardly bash him over the head on the bus or the train as both would have CCTV."

Sandra shook her head. "No, can't be the case. I mean, why would anyone splash out on travel expenses if they knew him back in Leeds?"

Zac helped himself to another portion of lasagne. "Can't be the case anyway because Garfield said the coppers told him that according to the bus driver, Lewis was the only person to get off in the village, so he couldn't have been followed."

"Might be that someone was waiting for him then," said Hetty, "You know, someone from Leeds who was already here on holiday perhaps and so someone else still in Leeds told the one down here he was on his way."

"Ouch, it makes my head ache trying to decipher that," chuckled Bill.

Hetty scowled. "What I'm trying to say is…oh never mind it's a daft notion anyway."

"Perhaps the motive was robbery," mused Lottie.

Sandra placed her knife and fork neatly on her empty plate. "But if that's the case, why hide his wallet and phone amongst the stones in the church wall?"

Lottie shrugged her shoulders. "No idea."

"And why not take the phone," said Hetty, "I mean it's probably worth a bob or two."

"Most likely because the police would be able to track it," said Emma.

"Not if they didn't know its number," reasoned Zac, "I mean with no means of identification on his person when he was found, the police would know nothing about him."

"Oh, well, I suppose it'll all get sorted one day," Sandra topped up her wine glass.

"Not necessarily," said Kate, "Lots of cases are never solved and to date this one seems to have no clues."

"Hmm, talking of dates, I nearly forgot," Emma took hold of Zac's hand, "We've seen Vicar Sam and have yet another date for our wedding and hopefully this one will go ahead."

"Wonderful," Sandra's eyes sparkled, "so when is it?"

"Saturday September the seventeenth," said Zac, "Needless to say, the ceremony will be in the church."

"And the reception in the grounds of Pentrillick House," Emma added.

"A year from now then," said Lottie, "so plenty of time to make plans."

Hetty agreed, "I just hope this wretched pandemic is history by then."


After lunch, Sandra loaded up the dishwasher and Kate and Vicki made tea and coffee for everyone. To keep out of the way, other family members went into the sitting room to relax by the fire.

"I like the glass baubles," said Lottie, pointing to two sets of three fishermen's balls hanging either side of the inglenook fireplace, "Very pretty and I love the way they reflect the flames in the fire."

"Sandra got them from the charity shop," said Bill, "Apparently they have loads and are left over stock from a gift shop in Penzance that's ceased trading."

"That's interesting. We've not been in the shop for a while, have we, Het."

"We have. We popped in briefly a while back because Maisie called us in to tell us about Willow Mackenzie. We didn't look round the shop though, so we really must have a browse if we can find the time."

"Find the time!" Bill chuckled, "I suppose you're too busy sleuthing to do anything else."

Hetty looked indignant. "Well, yes, we've had a discussion or two about the goings on here, I must admit, but we've not got ourselves into any scrapes if that's what you're trying to infer."

"Plenty of time for that yet," he teased.

Hetty picked up a cushion to throw at her nephew but decided against it when Sandra entered the room and took a seat beside her mother-in-law. The twins followed with a tray of hot drinks. After they'd drunk the beverages, all agreed they felt too lazy to even play board games and so settled down to watch a film; some saw it through from beginning to end and others glimpsed snippets in between catnaps.

As the film credits rolled, Hetty, stifling a yawn, glanced towards the window as Sandra stood up to draw the curtains. "I really ought to take Albert for a short walk before it gets dark."

"Well if you do I'll go with you. I could do with a bit of exercise after the amount I've eaten today and Crumpet could do with a walk too. He's getting fat. " Bill leaned forwards and plumped up the cushions in his chair.

"I don't think Crumpet wants a walk. To keep out of Mum's way, Kate and I took him for a good run this morning and he still looks knackered." Vicki gently stroked the small dog, sound asleep in his basket.

"Okay, but I still need to stretch my legs." Bill reached for his shoes.

Sandra stood up. "I'm feeling quite thirsty so I'm going to have another cup of tea. Does anyone else what one? We have blueberry muffins too. Kate made them and they're really delicious."

Hetty's face lit up. "Yes please, Sandra. That sounds lovely and so we'll go out after that," she glanced at her sister, "Will you come with us too, Lottie?"

"No, I don't think so. If you have Bill for company you'll not need me and I really don't fancy venturing with it being wet and miserable. Besides, I'm nice and comfortable here and as my shoes are new they're not worn-in yet."


It was a little after seven-thirty when Hetty and Bill left the Old Bakehouse. The streetlamps had just come on and the wet pavements and roads shone in their reflected light. As neither were feeling very energetic and the dark sky threatened more rain, they decided not to go far, just along the main street to the Crown and Anchor and then back again. They met no-one on the first leg of their walk and saw no traffic either but on their way back as they passed the church the Sharpe brothers' van drove along the street towards them. Hetty and Bill waved and the brothers waved back.

"Wonder where they've been," said Hetty. "It's too dark for cleaning windows."

"They could have been anywhere. The supermarket, fishing, playing golf, visiting someone. Really, the list is endless."

"Hmm," thoughts of going out reminded Hetty of the previous evening and visions of the cinema flashed across her mind; she was surprised to find herself thinking of Paul Fox and his suggestion of a joint birthday party.

"I wonder if he was serious," she muttered without thinking.

"You wonder if who was serious?" Bill asked.

"What? Oh, ignore me I was just thinking out loud."

Bill frowned but knowing his aunt, thought it best to say no more. They walked on in silence but when they were level with the fish and chip shop, Hetty spotted a notice in the window. Curious as to what it might say she insisted they cross the road to take a look. To her dismay it listed opening times for the winter months.

"Bill laughed at the disappointed look on Hetty's face. "Well, what did you expect it to say? Surely not an up-date on the state of Matilda's son?"

"I don't know what I expected, which is daft really. I suppose I'm just naturally a nosy parker."

"You said it," chuckled Bill.

However, as they levelled with the pasty shop, Hetty's curiosity rose again. She stopped walking and pointed to the shop's upstairs windows. "Look, someone is moving around up there. I just caught sight of a figure as it passed the chink of light between the curtains on the middle window."

Bill likewise stopped and looked to the upper storey of the building. There were three windows in all but chinks of light were only visible between the curtains of the central one. "Well, we know it's not Dennis or Jude because we've just seen them and it's hardly likely to be the girls."

"Exactly," Hetty quickly glanced in both directions and stepped onto the road, "Come on, Bill, we need to investigate."

"What! No way. I think we need to either ring the brothers or the police."

Hetty tutted. "We don't know the brothers' phone numbers and it'd be unfair to bother the police in the evening, especially if whoever's there is entitled to be so. What's more, by the time they got here, whoever is in there might have gone."

"But…"

"…No buts, come on, Billy."

"I really don't think it's wise."

Hetty looked back over her shoulder as she crossed the road and stepped onto the pavement. "You're not scared surely."

"Of course not." Bill ran across the road to catch up with his aunt."

"Good, because your mother wouldn't have hesitated." Hetty knew this was stretching the truth, for had Lottie been present her reaction would have been similar to that of her son.

By the kerb in front of the pasty shop stood a stationary white van but they considered it of no consequence as several other vehicles were parked along the street. Wondering if they might be able to hear voices inside the shop, they stood by the door and listened, but all was quiet.

"Let's go round the back," Hetty picked up Albert and led the way down a narrow alleyway. Half way along, she opened a solid wooden gate and they crept into the shop's rear courtyard beyond which lay a large walled garden, surrounded by the silhouette of trees and shrubs.

Hetty looked at a part-glazed UPVC door on the back of the building and tried the handle. It was unlocked and so she slowly pushed it open.

"Won't Albert bark?" Bill whispered.

Hetty shook her head, pulled a bag of doggy treats from her pocket, popped one into Albert's mouth and said quietly, "Shush boy."

Once inside, Bill gently closed the door and then on tip-toe they crept along a dark hallway. To their right was the kitchen; quiet except for the humming of fridges and freezers. And dark except for digital lights on the electrical equipment. Before they reached the door leading into the shop, they saw another door slightly ajar with a key its Yale lock. Hetty pushed it open and both peeped around it. On the other side was a large hallway, square in shape and lit by a solitary light bulb hanging from a shade-less cord. At the back of the hallway was a staircase. Quietly they stepped inside. With no windows and natural light it smelt musty. Paper hung from the walls both above and below a dark wooden dado rail. Brown paint peeled from the skirting boards and the bare treads on the winding staircase. The newel post at the foot of the stairs leaned to one side, clearly rotten at the base, and several banister rails were missing. Hetty and Bill quietly crept across the dirty tiled floor and at the bottom of the stairs stood and listened. Someone was definitely up there. Muffled voices could be heard along with footsteps on bare floorboards.

"What do we do?" Bill whispered.

"Wait and see who comes down. If we don't know them or they look dodgy we'll ring the police."

As she spoke a door on the upper floor opened and someone walked along the landing. Desperate not to be seen, Hetty and Bill dashed across the hall, crouched beneath the stairs and hid in the shadows. Both held their breath as heavy footsteps ran down the stairs and two men stepped into the hall carrying large plastic trays. They crossed the dirty floor and as the first man went out into the passageway, the second switched off the light. The Yale lock clicked into place as he closed the door. Brisk footsteps followed along the passageway. As Hetty and Bill crept out from their hiding place, they heard a key turn in the lock of the back door.

Bill stood up straight. "Great, now we're locked in." His voice was little more than a whisper.

Hetty bit her bottom lip. "That is a bit of a bugger," Albert growled and so she put him down. "Don't worry, boy. We'll get out." In the dark she felt for the Yale lock, opened the door, and stepped out into the dark passageway. Bill and Albert followed. Hetty tried to open the back door. It was definitely locked. She and Bill felt around the doorframe and the window sill; there was no sign of spare key.

"How about we try the shop door," Bill suggested.

"Good thinking."

They walked back along the passage and through an unlocked door leading into the shop. When they saw a Yale lock their spirits rose but they were unable to get out as the door was secured by a second lock. Hoping to find a spare key, they searched high and low but once again without success. Hetty swore beneath her breath.

Bill was more upbeat. "Never mind, we'll get out somehow. Meanwhile I suggest we take a look upstairs and see what's up there."

Back in the square hall, Bill switched on the light.

"Is that wise?" Hetty pointed to the dusty light bulb.

"There are no windows in here, so no-one will see from outside." Bill stepped onto the bottom tread of the stairs. "I'll go first just in case there's still someone up there."

"Okay but I don't think there is." Hetty cautiously followed Bill up the uncarpeted stairs aware of every sound on every tread. At the top they paused and looked along the dark landing. Chinks of light shone from beneath three of the four closed doors.

"Why've they left the lights on?" tutted Hetty.

"I've a sneaky feeling I know the answer to that. What can you smell?"

Hetty sniffed the air. "There's the musty smell from the hall downstairs and yes, there is something else as well but I've no idea what."

Bill reached for the knob of the first door. "I think you'll find it's going to be very warm in here." He opened the door.

"Plants," gasped Hetty, "Why on earth are they growing plants up here. They're all the same too so not very imaginative."

Bill chuckled. "They're all the same for a purpose, Aunt Het. They're cannabis plants."

"You mean?"

"Yes."

"Goodness me. So is this shop just a cover for dealing drugs because if it is, that's dreadful?"

Bill cast his eyes around the room. "The plants aren't very big so I'd imagine they're not mature yet. I'm afraid it's not really something I know much about."

"Nor me," Hetty ran her hand down one of the walls. It was running with condensation despite two dehumidifiers humming at either end of the room.

"Let's go and see if they've got it growing in the other rooms as well." Bill walked out onto the landing followed by Hetty and Albert. The set-up in the first was the same as the big room on the front, and although the plants were slightly bigger they looked sick and stunted. The second room was the same again except the plants beneath heated lamps were small seedlings. Because they looked fresh and healthy, Bill suggested the two men they had seen carrying trays might just have delivered them. The last room was empty.

"What are we going to do?" Hetty asked, as they returned to the first room, "The others will be getting worried if we're not back soon and we're locked in."

"Hmm, and this is hardly my idea of the perfect place to spend a Friday evening. I think we're going to have to ring for help because short of breaking a window there's no way out and we don't want to set off any alarms."

"But ring who? We can hardly call the police because if we do they'll nick us for breaking and entering even though the door was unlocked when we got here." Hetty shuddered at the thought of being arrested.

"I doubt it. Not when they see what we've uncovered."

"How about if I ring David and Margot then? It'd be much less painful than having strangers turn up waving their truncheons."

Bill chuckled. "Truncheons! I think you'll find they went out of favour years ago."

"Well, you know what I mean."

"I do and as for ringing David and Margot it seems unfair to disturb Dave if he's off duty."

"I don't think he'll mind too much and he might be at work anyway."

"Okay, I'll give Margot a ring because we exchanged numbers when we first became workmates." Bill scrolled through the list of contacts on his phone.

"Just as well you're doing it because I don't have their numbers anyway and even if I did my phone's back at your place in my bag."

While Bill rang Margot, Hetty walked between the rows of plants thinking how attractive the foliage was. "I wouldn't mind one of these as a house plant," she said as Bill ended the call and returned his phone to his pocket, "It looks like they're prone to green fly though as some of the leaves are smothered in them and there won't be any natural predators up here so the little blighters will thrive."

"I agree they're nice looking but it wouldn't be a good idea to grow one."

"Pity," Hetty broke off a leaf, inspected it for aphids and seeing it was clean, put it in her pocket to show to Lottie, "So what did Margot say?"

"She was shocked when I told her what we'd found but at the same time I think she thought it funny that we'd managed to get locked in. Anyway, she's about to tell David who isn't working tonight and he'll deal with it. So we just have to sit and wait."

"Thank goodness. Well, at least it's nice and warm in here. Meanwhile, I think you'd better ring Sandra and explain because we could be here some time."

But before Bill had a chance to make the call they heard a vehicle pull up outside the shop.

"That was quick," Hetty opened the door ready to welcome the police.

Bill frowned. "Too quick if you ask me."

"No, silly. David's only in Blackberry Way so it's no distance at all."

"But surely he'll report it before he gets here and wait for reinforcements."

"Reinforcements! No, Bill, not when it's just you, me and Albert."

On hearing his name, Albert barked.

Down below they heard the back door open and voices in the lower hallway. "That's not the police because the police don't have a key. Quick hide." Bill kicked the door shut.

Hetty looked around. "Hide. But where? There's nothing in here but plants and dehumidifiers and none will cover me."

Albert barked again as they heard the thudding of feet running up the stairs. The door opened and in sprang Dennis and Jude.

Jude lowered the cricket bat in his right hand. "Oh no. Not you, Mrs Tonkins."

"Miss Tonkins," corrected Hetty, "I've never been married."

"You don't surprise me there," chuckled Dennis.

"Shut it," snapped Jude.

"How did you know we were here?" Bill asked.

"Our mates sensed someone hiding in the hallway when they left so they rang us and suggested we checked it out," Dennis noticed the phone in Bill's hand, "Come on, give that to me." Bill handed it over and Dennis switched it off.

"One of them thought he could smell doggy treats too," Jude looked down at Albert who oblivious of the ensuing danger was sniffing around the plants."

"Damn," muttered Hetty.

"So what goes on here?" Bill thought it best to keep them talking until the police arrived.

Dennis tutted derisively. "Come on, man, it's pretty obvious, isn't it? We're trying to grow the stuff and when it's ready we'll to flog it on to dealers."

Hetty shook her head. "How could you, Jude? And to think I thought you were a nice couple of lads."

"We are, Miss Tonkins but we need to make a living and there's not much to be made cleaning windows. Having said that, we've not earned a penny from this stuff yet. I don't think we have green fingers and it's cost an arm and a leg to set it all up."

"Never mind what we're doing here and the rest of it. Why are you two here nosing around?" Dennis looked angry.

"We were out walking Albert," said Bill, "when we saw through a chink of light in the curtains someone moving around in here. We knew it wasn't you two because we'd just seen you drive by, so we thought you might have intruders."

"So you see, we actually thought we were doing you a favour," said Hetty, "The door was unlocked so we came in to investigate and heard someone moving around up here. When we heard whoever they were coming downstairs, we hid."

Dennis snorted. "Well for your information, we knew the blokes were here because we'd just let them in to deliver more plants and we had to give them some money. We couldn't hang around because Doll said dinner would be ready at eight and she gets ratty if we're late. So we left

142

them to put the plants in place and they said when they'd finished they'd lock up and put the key in its hiding place, like they've done before."

Hetty groaned. "So what are you going to do with us now we know what you're up to, Dennis?"

"Not sure. Let me think about it." Hetty didn't like the tone of his voice or the way he banged his fist into the palm of his hand.


Detective Inspector David Bray arrived outside the pasty shop at the same time as four work colleagues, but to avoid raising suspicion all drove further on along the road and parked outside the Old Bakehouse. For having seen the window cleaning van parked in front of the pasty shop, they thought it highly likely that the brothers had returned to the premises some time after Bill had spoken to the DI's wife on the phone.

Kate, in the kitchen unloading the dishwasher, heard the three vehicles pull up alongside the kerb; to see if they had unexpected visitors she looked from the dining room window. When she saw that two of the vehicles were police cars she excitedly reported it to the rest of the family. All went outside to take a look.

"That's David's car." Lottie pointed to her neighbour's silver BMW parked behind the two police vehicles.

"Are you sure, Grandma?" Vicki hoped it was.

"Yes, I recognise the number plate."

Sandra stepped out onto the quiet road and looked in both directions. "Weird, there's no-one about and I can't hear anything."

"Must be a domestic somewhere," reasoned Lottie, "Hopefully Het and Bill will see something while on their travels and be able to put us in the picture when they get back."

Sandra looked at her watch. "They've been gone rather a long time. I thought they were only going for a short walk." She rang Bill's mobile to make sure all was well but her call went straight onto voicemail.

After a nail-biting hour for the family, Hetty and Bill arrived back at the Old Bakehouse. Both looked flustered.

"Where on earth have you been?" Lottie asked before they had even closed the door, "We've been worried sick."

"And why have you turned your phone off, Bill?" Sandra snapped.

"More importantly," said Vicki, "have you any idea why there are police vehicles parked outside?"

"You'll never believe us when we tell you." Hetty unclipped Albert's lead and then flopped down in the nearest chair, "and yes, Vicki, we do know why there are police cars outside. In fact tomorrow, your dad and I have to attend the police station in Camborne to make statements."

"The police station!" Feeling faint, Lottie sat down quickly. "Good gracious me! What have you done now, Het?"

"Not a lot. Just apprehended two villains."

"Two villains?" Sandra squeaked.

"Wow! Cool!" giggled Vicki.

"It's rather a long story, love." Bill unzipped his jacket and took a crisp from a dish on the table, "Give us a minute to unwind and then we'll explain."

Vicki sniffed the air. "I can smell...no surely not." Seeing the amused expressions on her father and great aunt's faces, she cast them a questioning look.

"Before we say anything, your aunt and I need a drink," Bill opened a can of lager for himself and poured Hetty a glass of wine.

"Thank you," Hetty reached for the proffered glass and took several large gulps, "That's better, I really needed that."

"So what's happened? Come on, we're itching to know." Sandra sat down beside her husband, and then between them Hetty and Bill told of the illicit goings on at the pasty shop, the brothers turning up and finally the arrival of the police.

"Good gracious. You can't even take the dog for a walk without getting into a scrape, can you, Het?" Lottie tried to be severe.

Bill chuckled.

"And you're no better, William," scolded Sandra, "You could have been killed."

"Well, I think it's hilarious," said Vicki, "Can't wait to get back to uni and tell my friends."

"But what's it all about?" Sandra asked, "I mean, did the four of them buy the shop just to grow weed or did they buy the shop to sell pasties and then the idea of becoming growers cropped up? I'd love to know."

"Cropped up," giggled Vicki, "Good one, Mum."

Sandra scowled at her daughter.

"Well, I'm sure we'll find out in due course," Hetty drained her glass and Vicki refilled it.

Kate, who sat on the hearth rug with legs crossed quietly sipping a gin and tonic, tipped her head to one side. "It's just a thought, but do any of you think it's possible that like you, Dad and Auntie Het, Eddie discovered the stuff growing upstairs. I mean if he did and the brothers found out that he knew, they'd want to shut him up, wouldn't they?"

Bill placed his empty can on the coffee table by his knees. "Good heavens, Kate, I reckon you're onto something there. In all the excitement I'd completely forgotten about young Eddie."

"And it's a lot better a motive than Dennis silencing Eddie permanently because he'd spotted him with a wealthy blonde," said Lottie.

"A wealthy blonde!" Bill spluttered, "What on earth are you talking about, Mum?"

"Oh dear, silly me. We'd agreed not to mention it, hadn't we, Het?"

"We had but I don't think it matters now."

Hetty briefly explained that Dennis had been spotted on two occasions with the blonde divorcee who they knew to be a wealthy widow called Caroline Bates.

"Hmm, I can see why you might have suspected him then," acknowledged Sandra, "but going back to the pasty shop doings, I can't believe that Dolly and Eve could be involved in anything as sinister as murder and I know for a fact they both liked young Eddie."

Lottie nodded. "I'm inclined to agree, Sandra. The girls are lovely and so I hope it turns out that neither of them knew what was going on upstairs. Although if I'm honest I find that hard to believe."

"Jude's a nice lad too," said Hetty, "although the same can't be said for Dennis now we know he's a two-timing rat who, had the police not arrived when they did, might have murdered Bill and me." She shuddered at the thought.

"But you must admit it makes sense regardless of whether or not Dolly and Eve knew what was going on. The pasty shop mob are the only ones with a motive because no-one else really knew Eddie that well." Kate was convinced they were on the right track.

"Hang on a minute. I mean, we don't know for sure that Eddie was murdered," Sandra reminded them all, "as far as I know there's no evidence to suggest it was anything other than a tragic accident."

"I agree with Mum," said Vicki, "it must have been an accident because those two pasty shop women wouldn't hurt a fly."

"We're not suggesting they've hurt anyone, we're pointing our fingers at their blokes, the brothers. What's more, there is a slim chance the girls didn't know about the cannabis because the door into the hall where the stairs are is kept locked. Anyway there's only one way to find out." Bill pulled out his phone and once again phoned Margot to relay their latest thoughts. When he ended the call he turned to the family and smiled. "Great minds think alike because they're already on the case."

# Chapter Nineteen

The discovery of the cannabis plants caused the police to review the death of Eddie Madigan. For up until that point they had come across no-one with a motive for murder nor any witnesses having seen suspicious activity around the scene of the crime other than the two girls from Sheffield who saw someone inside Eddie's caravan on the night he disappeared and then again the following evening shortly before he was reported missing by James Dale, the landlord of the Crown and Anchor.

Following their arrest, Jude and Dennis Sharpe were questioned separately but both had refused to co-operate, and so later that evening, two police cars arrived at Fuchsia Cottage and Eve and Dolly were taken in for questioning. Meanwhile, down in the village, the pasty shop, a crime scene, was taped off, a police officer was placed outside, and the premises was forcibly closed for the foreseeable future.

On arriving at the police station, Eve and Dolly were taken into separate rooms and interviewed individually. Both told identical stories. That the four of them had jointly bought the premises to open up as a pasty shop and then when they had sufficient funds they would renovate the upstairs rooms so they could live there. However, after a while Dennis talked them into growing cannabis to speed up their savings by claiming there was good money to be had. At first, Eve and Dolly had been very much against the idea, saying it was immoral, but after Jude was won over they too finally succumbed and the cannabis farm went ahead. The police, sensing that Eve was likely to be more forthcoming than Dolly, interviewed her for a second time after they had compared notes. When asked if Eddie had known of the plants upstairs, she said no, he never went up there because Dennis had told him that the staircase was unsafe. She was then asked if on the last day Eddie was seen alive and was alone in the shop, she thought it possible he might have slipped upstairs to take a look around. Eve thought it unlikely because to make sure no unauthorised person went up there, Dennis had fitted a Yale lock and the door was kept shut. However, she admitted the key wasn't very well hidden. In fact it wasn't hidden at all. Because it was a small key, Dennis kept it on top of the door frame out of sight but easy enough for anyone to find if they ran their hand along the top of the frame. This caused her to admit it was possible that on the last day Eddie had worked in the shop, he might have found the key and taken a look upstairs, despite the fact he was only left alone for a short while. The reason the girls had left him alone was they needed to get groceries and as the shop was quiet they knew he would be okay. It never crossed their minds that he might go snooping because he was always glad to get away at closing time and never hung around. When they arrived at work the following morning, they found he'd posted the shop keys through the letterbox as instructed, hidden the till drawer in the paper bag cupboard and activated the alarm. The hall door was locked and there was nothing to suggest he'd been up there. Furthermore, Eve insisted he wouldn't have hung around because it was common knowledge that he planned to meet up with Dee for a music session.

"What time did you get back with your shopping?" Detective Inspector David Bray asked Eve.

She sighed. "Just before seven. No, it was seven because I heard the church clock strike as we were unloading the car. We can hear it quite clearly when the wind's in the south west."

"And were Dennis and Jude already home?"

"Yes, they usually get back just after half five about the same as us. So I assume they'd been there since then."

"You assume but you don't know."

"Well no, of course not. I mean, we had no reason to ask."

"Were they acting as normal?"

"I suppose so. They said they'd got two new clients and seemed pleased about that. Oh, and they kept tittering too but wouldn't tell us the joke."

"And they never said anything that puzzled you or made you suspicious?"

"No, but…" Eve frowned.

"What is it?"

"Well, it's just that the following morning, Dolly and I were in the shop kitchen and while Dolly was glazing the first batch of pasties, I left her to it and went out into the hallway to collect the till drawer from the paper bag cupboard, put there as I said by Eddie the night before. Anyway, when I went out there Dennis was on his phone and I overheard him say," She paused, "now let me get this right, he said, something like, 'don't worry we managed to delete them'. Then he saw me and said: 'Anyway, must go, Mum. Love to Dad and I'll ring you again soon'."

"And why did that make you suspicious?"

"Because it was ten past eight in the morning. I mean, Dennis and Jude's parents are in their seventies and so why would he phone them that early? He doesn't usually."

"Perhaps they phoned him?"

"No, because he said I'll ring you again soon, so surely he must have rung them."

"So you don't think he was talking to his mother at all?"

"No, but then. Oh, I don't know. It's all so confusing."

"Do you know if there has ever been a CCTV system in the upstairs rooms?"

"What! No, well, not as far as I know. I mean, why would there be?" Eve sat up straight, "Oh no, you think if there was Dennis or Jude might have seen Eddie up there."

"I do, because there is evidence of a camera having been there, but it's not there now so we can only assume it might have been removed after Eddie disappeared."

"Meaning, if they knew he'd been up there, then that'd give them a motive to..." her words faded.

Following the interviews, Eve and Dolly were released late on Friday night without charge pending further enquiries. Jude and Dennis remained under arrest but after no sleep both simultaneously agreed on Saturday morning to co-operate and tell their version of events providing a solicitor was present.


Hetty and Lottie, having talked endlessly of Eddie's case, were in the front garden of Primrose Cottage, glad of a distraction as they planned how to achieve the 'wow' factor needed to enter the Pentrillick in Bloom competition in 2022. The meeting planned for Saturday morning with Debbie and Kitty to discuss the outcome of their visit to Penzance had been postponed until Sunday afternoon to give Hetty time to recover from her ordeal in the upstairs rooms of the pasty shop.

As they weeded a flower bed in front of the house, having decided to plant a strongly scented climbing rose against the wall, they saw Eve slowly ambling along Blackberry Way; her eyes were red from crying.

"Are you alright, Eve love?" Lottie could clearly see she wasn't but it seemed only right to ask.

Eve nodded. "Yes. Well, no. The thing is, they've been charged and I just can't believe either of them would have done it. I couldn't sleep last night and so went to the police station this morning and asked if I could see Jude but they said no. I was distraught because I wanted him to tell me exactly what happened the day Eddie disappeared. The police were nice enough and said the brothers were co-operating now but at this stage a visit couldn't be allowed. They gave me the name of their solicitor though and so in desperation I rang him when I got back to my car and he briefly told me of Jude's account, but it seems the police don't believe him even though his version of the event is exactly the same as told by Dennis."

"Would you like to come in for a cup of tea?" Hetty asked, "They say it's good to talk."

"Yes, please, I'd like that." She walked towards the gate, "I'm on my own because Dolly's gone shopping. We need milk and bread you see. Not that we have much appetite."

When all were seated in the sitting room, the sisters, not wanting to rush their young guest, made small talk about the weather, the Corona Virus and the Pentrillick in Bloom competition.

Eve half smiled. "When we heard about that we thought we'd enter it. The shop category, that is. It'd look nice with a few tubs and hanging baskets out the front. Now I'm not so sure. I mean, I don't know if we'll be here next year or if we'll ever open up again."

"I'm sure you will," said Lottie.

"I hope so but I don't really see how it'll be viable. Our expenses will be huge and without the boys' income we'll not be able to afford the rent let alone the mortgage. What's more, Dolly and me will most likely face criminal charges. Aiding and abetting the growing of illicit goods or something like that, even though we were always dead against it and it's not made us a penny."

"You knew then," Hetty felt disappointed, "We'd hoped it was done without your knowledge."

"Yes, we knew although it was not on the cards when we first got the shop. In retrospect though it was probably always the reason Dennis wanted to buy the place. I certainly remember his enthusiasm when we saw the upstairs rooms but I thought his keenness was just for the potential accommodation. I've since learned he knew someone who grew the ghastly stuff before we moved down here and that's why he was keen to try it out. Although I don't think either of the brothers have green fingers because the first batch they bought as seedlings died and the other day they said the next lot are looking pretty sick too. I must admit I was quite relieved and hoped they'd give up the idea. What's more, it's costing a fortune to keep buying new seedlings as you can't just pop along to the garden centre," She glanced towards the window as a car drove by, "Oh, it's your neighbours. I thought it might be Dolly coming back. I don't know what time she went though. I wasn't here whenever it was because I'd already gone to the police station, then after I rang the solicitors I went and sat in a park for ages to think things out. When I got back home I found a note saying she'd gone shopping. To calm my nerves I put the kettle on for tea or whatever but before it'd boiled, the lads' solicitor rang to tell me they've just been charged. So I had to get out of the house." She hung her head, "I feel like I'm in a nightmare."

"So what exactly have they been charged with?" Hetty asked.

"Murder, would you believe?"

"Oh dear," despite her earlier protestations, Hetty hoped they and the police had jumped to the wrong conclusion.

"Perhaps I ought to start at the beginning and tell you what the solicitor told me."

Lottie bit her bottom lip. "You don't have to do this, Eve. We don't want you to be any more upset than you already are."

"Oh, but I must. As you said it's good to talk and I'd rather people knew the truth than jumped to outrageous conclusions."

"Yes, some gossipy people around here are apt to do just that." Hetty felt her face flush on realising that she fell into the category mentioned.

Lottie rolled her eyes. "Never a truer word spoken, Het."

Recalling mention of the ladies' sleuthing efforts, Eve managed a half smile then proceeded to tell her news. "On the day Eddie disappeared the lads, having finished work, headed for home around half five and while Jude drove, Dennis checked his phone for messages and what have you. He then looked at the CCTV in the upper rooms of the shop, which I might add I knew nothing about, and to his horror saw Eddie up there taking pictures of the plants on his phone. And so instead of coming straight home, when they got to the village they drove to the pasty shop but Eddie by then had gone and locked up. So they drove back through the village and Jude dropped Dennis off at the pub so he could confront Eddie. Jude then drove home because they didn't want to intimidate the lad by both being there. Anyway, Dennis went to the caravan but Eddie wasn't there. He arrived shortly after though carrying booze and crisps. After he'd unlocked the door they both went inside and Dennis confronted him about the pictures he'd taken. At first Eddie denied it, but when Dennis grabbed Ed's phone and found the pictures, Eddie laughed, said sorry and that he meant no harm. He thought it was cool, you see, to have such goings on in a pasty shop of all places and just wanted to show them to his mates when he eventually went home. He also let it be known that even though he disapproved of drug use, he'd never have reported it because of the negative publicity it'd attract. Dennis believed him, but to be on the safe side he deleted the pictures. Eddie was alright about it and according to Dennis, was alive and well when he left the caravan and walked back home to Fuchsia Cottage. The reason Eddie was alone in the shop to lock up and so forth was so that Dolly and me could get away early to go shopping. We got home at seven. Both lads were there and everything was normal."

"And the police don't believe them?" said Hetty.

"No, and to be honest I can see their point."

"So what do the police claim happened?" Lottie asked.

"They reckon either Dennis or both of them confronted Ed as they've admitted but that Eddie felt threatened and was scared. This caused him to run off towards the cliff path where one or both of the brothers caught up with him and they pushed him over the edge. They reckon the brothers then wiped their fingerprints off Eddie's phone and went home. Which is absolute nonsense. I'd have known if they'd killed someone. They're not good actors. In fact in retrospect they were in good humour when we got home that day. They wouldn't tell us why but I should imagine it was because they were amused by Ed's laughter at cannabis plants being grown over a pasty shop."

"Oh, dear," sighed Lottie, "what can we do to help?"

Hetty ran her hand through her hair. "There's only one thing we can do. We have to find out who the real culprit is."

"But we've already tried and got nowhere," gasped Lottie.

"Then we'll have to try harder. The police won't bother looking now if they think they've got the right people and so it's all down to us."

# Chapter Twenty

"Have you thought any more about the two girls staying with Norman and Jackie?" Debbie asked, after arriving on Sunday afternoon for the meeting postponed from the previous day. "I ask because someone at Pentrillick House told Gideon that a couple of girls were seen skulking on the pub field a while back and they felt they were up to no good."

Hetty frowned. "Well, no because they told us they used to lurk on the field to spy on Eddie so as far as I'm concerned there's nothing more to think about."

Debbie looked over the rim of the spectacles she wore ready to read an article in the Pentrillick Gazette regarding the Hamiltons' stay in the village. "Yes, I know that but we only have their word for it, don't we? I mean, perhaps they just said they were spying on him in case they were seen. Remember they come from his area and so probably had reason to bear a grudge."

"I think you have a good point there," agreed Lottie, "Can you check them out on Facebook, Het."

"I suppose so." Hetty took her phone from the coffee table, logged onto Facebook and clicked on *search*. "Damn! I can't look them up, can I? Because I don't know either of their surnames."

Debbie sighed. "And there will be dozens, no hundreds if not thousands, of Lucys and Gemmas."

"Jackie and Norman must know their surnames," reasoned Kitty, "perhaps we could ring them."

Hetty slid her phone back on the table. "I think it might be better if we go and see them. If we phone they'll wonder why and we need to be subtle."

"Shall we go today then? Gideon's gone fishing with Robert Oliver so I've nothing else to do."

Hetty nodded. "Yes, it's good to strike while the iron's hot so we'll go later this afternoon, because whatever anyone says, I think Jude's a good lad even if he did get himself mixed up with illegal drugs and I'll move heaven and earth to get justice for them both."

"Even two-timing Dennis?" Lottie laughed.

"Yes, even two-timing Dennis."

"Well, you'll have to count me out," said Kitty, "because I'm playing the organ in church tonight and I don't want anything untoward to happen and make me late, but I wish you all the best of luck."


At half past three, Debbie, Hetty and Lottie left Primrose Cottage and walked to Cobblestone Close. They found the girls at home with Jackie. Norman was out having gone to Penzance to get a new battery for his van.

"Have you heard any more news about Matilda's son's memory?" Jackie asked, as the ladies sat, "It's just people talk about it in the pub and I wondered if he's been able to remember anything else."

"Not as far as we know," said Lottie, "but he's recovering from his injuries and should be out of hospital soon, so that's something."

"He'll probably never remember everything," said Debbie, "Which is a shame because whoever attacked him will get off scot-free."

"Talking of injuries. How's your ankle, Lucy?" Lottie observed Lucy was wearing shoes and her foot was not resting on the stool.

"As good as better, thanks. In fact we're hoping to go home on Wednesday. I should be going back to uni tomorrow but I've let them know about my foot and they're going to give me some work to do on-line so that I can keep up with the others. If all goes well I'll only miss the first week anyway."

"Will you be able to drive alright?" Hetty asked, "I mean, it's quite a long way."

"Yeah, I'll be fine and we'll make several stops so I can rest."

"You ladies missed a good evening in the pub last night," said Jackie, "The Hamiltons were in. At least Angie and Drake were. Bentley and Serena have gone back to London for a couple of days to sort something out. Drake had a brilliant time playing pool with the team who were in practicing, and Angie sat with the locals in the bar and charmed them with her presence. What with that and the chat over the goings on in the upstairs rooms of the pasty shop, the atmosphere was buzzing. James said the takings were well above the average for a Saturday night in September."

"Damn! We nearly popped down, didn't we, Het, seeing as there was nothing on TV but we decided against it as you'd no doubt have been bombarded with questions."

"You certainly would have," agreed Jackie, "and no doubt you'd have been able to put a few facts straight."

Hetty smiled. "In a way I'd like to have been there but apart from not wanting to be interrogated, we didn't really have the energy because we'd been gardening all afternoon."

"Gardening. Yes, that reminds me. While you're here I'd like your opinion on something," Jackie leapt up to her feet and then pulled two sheets of card from behind the sofa, "Lucy is studying landscaping and garden design at uni and as a thank you for us looking after her she's very

158

kindly drawn up two plans for our back garden which currently is an unimaginative mess. Norman and me love them both, so it'd be nice to see what you all think."

"That's sounds exciting," Lottie took the first card and the three ladies studied it carefully. They then did the same with the second. After a fifteen minute deliberation they were unanimous that by a very slim margin they preferred the second.

Lucy clapped her hands with glee. "That's my favourite too."

"Ideal, so that's the one we'll go for. Norman will be pleased a decision has been made. Thank you, ladies." Jackie returned the cards to their safe place behind the sofa.

"Our pleasure," said Lottie, "I feel privileged to have been asked and I should imagine you have a glowing future ahead of you, Lucy. You're clearly very talented."

Lucy beamed. "Thank you."

"So what's your subject, Gemma?" Hetty asked.

"What, oh, um, media studies," she looked down at the floor as she answered and Hetty got the impression she considered her subject inferior.

"Well I wish you luck with that," said Debbie, "but with the internet and countless news channels, I think newspapers are fast becoming history."

"True, but then reporters and what have you are still needed for the internet and news channels, aren't they?" After the compliments they had paid Lucy, Lottie felt it only fair to encourage Gemma.

"Yes, I suppose you're right," conceded Debbie, "but I think a lot of the news on-line is copied and pasted."

"Most likely," Hetty addressed the girls, "Now, before you two go home, we must ask if you've been able to remember anything else about the person you saw on the pub field? We didn't want to bother you again but two of our neighbours have been charged with Eddie's murder and we don't think they did it."

"Yes, Jackie told us about that and she said they seemed really nice chaps," Lucy spoke with sympathy.

Gemma shuddered. "Must be horrible to be accused of something you know you didn't do."

"Quite," said Hetty.

"So have you remembered anything else?" Debbie was keen to pursue the subject.

The girls looked at each other. "Well there is one more thing which we didn't mention before because we felt guilty," Lucy didn't elaborate but sat twiddling a loose strand of hair around her finger. Gemma, noting the three ladies were wide-eyed in anticipation, took over. "It was the first night when we saw someone running across the field, who at the time we thought was Eddie. Anyway, something dropped from the person running's pocket. When he was out of sight we nipped over to see what it was hoping for a souvenir but it was just a half-eaten packet of wine gums."

Lottie gasped. "Do you still have them? I'm thinking of fingerprints."

Gemma shook her head. "Sadly not and that's why we feel guilty, isn't it, Luce? We ate them, you see. Because as I said, we thought they'd been dropped by Eddie. We threw the wrapper in the bin."

Hetty sighed. "And the bin will have long been emptied."

"Yes, and that's why we didn't tell the police when they questioned us. We thought we might get into trouble."

"Well, I suppose even that bit of information's something," chuckled Lottie, "Meaning we're looking for someone who likes wine gums."

"Not much help though, is it?' said Debbie, "I mean, for a start I like wine gums even though I've not had any for ages."

"Me too," agreed Lottie.

Jackie giggled. "Same for me although I prefer the real thing."

"Perhaps we could ask in the shop if they've sold any lately," Hetty suggested, "and if they have, to whom?"

"We could if we were the police," laughed Debbie, "but as civilians definitely not and it's unlikely they'd be able to tell us anyway. I mean, the gums must have been bought two or three weeks ago."

Lottie tutted. "And it's no good telling the police hoping they'll look into it because they think they've got the right people."

"Which is daft," said Jackie, "Certainly several people in the pub think the brothers are guilty but I don't and neither do the pool team members, especially now Jude is one of them."

"If they think the lads are guilty they should speak to poor Eve. The girl is distraught and I believe every word she told us."

Lottie nodded. "I agree, Het, because if she wasn't telling the truth she's a damn good actress."

"It's only just occurred to me," said Debbie, "but why did the wine gum eater go back to the caravan the night after Eddie disappeared?"

"We've asked ourselves that," said Gemma, "and we reckon he must have been looking for something."

"Or maybe it was to wipe away any fingerprints he left the night before," reasoned Jackie, "I mean, Eddie was only missing then and so whoever it was probably wanted to make sure he'd left no fingerprints before the body was found and the police showed up."

Hetty shook her head. "But it can't be the case because James picked up Eddie's phone when Dolly rang to see

161

why Eddie hadn't turned up for work the following morning, and according to Tess his prints were still on the phone, so had someone gone back the second night to wipe it clean, James' fingerprints wouldn't have been there either."

"Good point," agreed Debbie, "besides which, whoever had just pushed Eddie off the cliffs would have made sure all fingerprints were wiped that night and certainly not wait until the next day."

"He must have been looking for something then," reasoned Lottie, "Maybe he dropped something incriminating. A bank card, a bus ticket, a pen. The sky really is the limit."

At five o'clock, the ladies, realising that Jackie had to be at work at six, decided to leave. As they left the house, after wishing the girls a safe journey home, and started to walk back towards the road, Lottie sighed deeply, "Well, at least we know now that it definitely wasn't Dennis the girls saw."

"Why do you say that? I mean, as much as I want to believe it, it still could have been him." Hetty was surprised by her sister's sudden conviction.

"No, it couldn't because Lucy and Gemma's version of what happened on the night Eddie went missing doesn't fit in with Eve's explanation of Dennis's movements. The timeline isn't right."

Hetty scowled. "What do you mean?"

"According to the girls, on the first night they saw someone leave the caravan shortly before a second person, who we know to be Dee, arrived. But we know Dee didn't get there until half sevenish and according to Eve, Dennis was home long before then so it couldn't have been him. What's more, on the second night, the girls claim someone was inside the caravan and when he saw them, he shouted and they ran away. That's when Lucy hurt her ankle. But it couldn't have been Dennis because Eve told us that

Dennis deleted the phone pictures after confronting Eddie, so he had no reason to return a second time."

Hetty's jaw dropped. "Well, that's good enough for me. Without question Dennis is innocent and Jude wasn't even there."

"So," asked Debbie, "Who was the mystery person?"

Hetty shrugged her shoulders. "Goodness only knows. On the other hand, perhaps the girls aren't telling the truth. They might have made the whole thing up. What's more, we forgot to ask them their surnames."

"No, they must be telling the truth," said Lottie, "otherwise, they wouldn't have been able to describe Dee's movements on the night Eddie disappeared so accurately."

"Very true," admitted Hetty.

"So, if the girls are telling the truth, it looks like it's all down to us finding someone who likes wine gums," Debbie chuckled.

"And someone with a clumpy walk," Lottie reminded them, "Remember one of the girls, I can't recall which, said the person nipping across the pub field couldn't have been Willow because she's dainty and the person they saw had a clumpy walk."

The ladies walked on in silence each thinking how best to move their investigation forwards. When they reached the Crown and Anchor, Debbie suggested they call in for drinks and take them onto the pub's field to get a feel of what might have happened on the night Eddie went missing. Hetty and Lottie agreed and so each with a glass of wine in hand they made their way to a bench in the field and sat looking towards the caravan. But for all their thinking, reasoning and hypotheses, none was able to come up with a solution to the matter in hand.

# Chapter Twenty-One

"I wonder. Do you sell wine gums?" Hetty, in the village shop for a loaf of bread, noticed Miriam, the shop's proprietor, stocking up the sweet racks and asked on impulse.

"Sorry, Hetty we don't. We've got fruit gums, jellied fruit, jelly babies, fruit pastilles, lemon sherbet and lemon drops but not wine gums."

"Oh, that's a shame."

The shopkeeper pointed to bags of sweets hanging from pegs. "We also have boiled sweets. They're very popular and have a real fruity flavour."

"Hmm...yes and thank you for your help but I really wanted wine gums. Never mind, I'll get a bottle of merlot instead." Hetty wandered off to the wines, beers and spirits section leaving a very confused shopkeeper scratching her head.

"Well," said Hetty, two hours later as she sat in the living room at Primrose Cottage with Lottie, Debbie and Kitty, "at least we know the person who dropped the wine gums on the pub field didn't buy them in the village and so it's quite likely that the person in question is not a local."

"Oh, come on, Het," sighed Lottie, "just because they weren't bought in the village doesn't mean the person we're interested in doesn't come from here. Most people go into Penzance for their main shop and that includes us."

"True, I suppose and I daresay most supermarkets sell wine gums."

"Exactly and there's nothing to be gained from finding out which ones."

"In that case we need to find out who likes them rather than who bought them."

Kitty chuckled. "Good luck with that, Het."

"I agree," said Lottie, "I mean, we can hardly go up to people and bluntly ask them."

"I suppose we could pretend we're doing a survey," Hetty suggested.

Debbie shook her head. "No, because we'd have to ask lots of questions not just 'do you like wine gums?', and that would make it too complicated."

"What's more, everyone in the village knows us," said Lottie, "and they'd think it suspicious."

"But we don't need to question everyone, just our suspects."

Debbie tried to suppress the desire to laugh, "But we don't have any suspects, Het."

"We do. Gibson Bailey. I reckon he's a phoney and have said so all along even if he did make a fool of me with my Leonardo Riccioni ploy. He's quite chubby too so I bet he likes sweets."

"Maybe he does, Het, but he's not here to question now," Lottie reminded her, "and he doesn't fit the description given by Gemma and Lucy either. What's more, he gave you a book so you ought to think more kindly of him."

"He could wear padding so we'd not suspect him and remember he was staying in the pub when Eddie went missing so he was quite near to the murder scene." Hetty was desperate. "And as regards the book, he might have given me that so we'd think he was kind and generous."

Lottie ignored her sister's ramblings. "I wonder if either Jude or Dennis like wine gums. I mean, if we could establish that neither of them do, then it'd back up our theory that they had absolutely nothing to do with Eddie's death."

"Very good point," agreed Kitty, "and were that the case I think it'd be good enough evidence to pass on to the police. I'll call in on my way home and ask the girls. I need to see them anyway because I was discussing their situation with Tommy last night and we've agreed to let them off paying rent for the rest of the year while they sort their lives out."

"That's very magnanimous of you both. Well done." Lottie was impressed.

Debbie and Hetty agreed.

"Well we can afford it. We don't need much now as we seldom go anywhere so the rent is just pocket money really." Kitty stood up and reached for her handbag, "As you'll be wanting to know what the wine gum outcome is, I'll pop along there now and then come back and tell you."

To pass the time while Kitty was away the ladies discussed their hopes for normality to return before the year was out. As Debbie was saying how she and Gideon hoped to be able to go abroad in 2022 to celebrate their ruby wedding anniversary, Kitty returned. As she entered the room and flopped down in the chair she had recently vacated, the other three ladies noted she looked flustered but all refrained from saying so.

"Well," said Kitty, as she regained her breath, "I really don't know how to put this but it appears that Dennis likes wine gums."

"What!" gasped Hetty, "but that's terrible."

"How on earth did you find that out?" Debbie asked.

"Well, only Eve was there because Dolly had gone down to the pasty shop to make sure everything was alright. Anyway, I told her about the rent business and bless her she actually cried and as she mopped her eyes I suddenly remembered I had a bag of mints in my handbag so I took them out and offered her one to get onto the subject of sweets and it worked. She told me that she has a weakness for lemon sherbets and Dolly loves chocolate eclairs. Jude on the other hand prefers savoury stuff. Having got her talking I asked if Dennis was a savoury nut too and she said," Kitty paused to get her breath, "she said, since he gave up smoking, Dennis loves all sorts of sweets but his passion at the moment is wine gums."

Lottie shivered. "So it looks as though the lads might well be guilty after all."

"No, not Jude. No way," Hetty shook her head, "Remember he didn't go to the caravan to confront Eddie. He drove the van home and left it to Dennis, so he'd have believed what his brother told him."

Debbie's face was devoid of colour. "What do we do? I mean this is incriminating evidence against Dennis, so we ought to tell the police."

"Well I'm not doing it," Hetty was adamant.

"And I can't," said Kitty, "It'd be a terrible betrayal of trust."

Lottie held up her hands. "Don't look at me."

"Perhaps we could do it anonymously," said Debbie, "You know, ring them up and withhold the number or even write a note and post it."

"I propose we give it twenty-four hours," said Hetty, "and then if there have been no further developments we do as Debbie suggests and ring anonymously."

Lottie looked at the clock. "That gives us until ten minutes past twelve on Wednesday. Let's hope something happens before then."


On Wednesday morning, Lucy and Gemma placed their belongings into the back of Lucy's van and after

167

saying goodbye to Norman and Jackie, drove out of Cobblestone Close. However, before leaving the village they planned to call in at the pub for lunch because Lucy wanted to treat Gemma for looking after her.

Jackie, who wasn't due to work until the evening decided to make use of the dry sunny weather forecast for the following day and wash the bedding in the girls' room so that she could hang it out first thing in the morning. After stripping the twin beds she knelt down to look underneath to make sure the girls had left nothing behind: a habit she'd had ever since as a fourteen year old she'd left her favourite shoes beneath the bed in holiday accommodation in Wales while with her parents. To her surprise there was something there. A rectangular box. Jackie pulled the box out and lifted the lid. Inside was a mouth organ and engraved on its side was the name Eddie. As she recalled Eddie's mother asking if anyone had seen his mouth organ, Jackie flopped down on the bed before her legs gave way. It had to be Eddie's, but why was it under the bed Gemma had slept in? A quick glance at the clock told her the girls would still be in the pub. At the bottom of the stairs she shouted to Norman in the kitchen watering plants on the windowsill. "Just popping down the pub for something, Norm. Won't be long." Norman heard the front door slam shut. Surprised by her hasty exit he put down the watering can and went into the sitting room, where from the window he watched Jackie running down the close clutching something in her hand.


That same morning, while Lottie was at home making green tomato chutney, Hetty was out walking Albert. As she approached the Crown and Anchor, Gibson Bailey's car swept by and drove into the pub's car park. Surprised by his return, she paused and waited until he stepped from his car to make sure he was the driver.

"I thought it was you. Nice to see you again." Hetty wondered why he was back.

"And to see you too. Did you read the book?"

"Yes, I did thank you and so did my sister and a few of our friends. It's in the charity shop now though, so even more people can enjoy it."

"Good to hear." Gibson locked the car.

"So would it be rude to ask what brings you back again so soon?" Hetty eagerly asked.

"Not at all. It's to do with young Eddie's case. I rang James last night to see if there had been any developments and he told me the boyfriends of the pasty shop girls had been charged with murder but there was growing opinion in the village that they're innocent. So because I have something that might be of use to the police I booked myself a room and here I am."

Hetty's eyebrows shot up. "Whatever do you have?"

"I'll show you. I'd like a second opinion anyway." Gibson opened the boot of his car and removed his travel bag; from it he pulled a large brown envelope. As he unsealed it, Jackie ran into the car park, red-faced and out of breath.

"My goodness, are you alright, Jackie?" Hetty offered her arms to help steady the twenty-four year old.

"Yeah, I'm fine. It's just these slippers are rubbish for running in so it made it doubly hard work."

Hetty, puzzled by Jackie's inappropriate footwear, led her to a low wall and suggested she sit to get her breath back.

Gibson nodded to the box in Jackie's hand. "Is that a harmonica? I recognise the brand name."

Jackie nodded. "Yes, it is. I found it under Gemma's bed and I've come down to see why she has it. It belongs to Eddie, you see. So unless he gave it to her, she must have taken it from his caravan."

169

Hetty frowned. "So where are the girls now? I mean, I thought they were going home today."

"They are, but they said they wanted to pop in the pub for lunch before they left. That's why I'm here. To apprehend them and they've not gone yet because that's Lucy's van over there."

Gibson's usually ruddy face turned pale. "I think we need to take this calmly and perhaps get the police here."

"Police. Why?" Hetty was struggling to make sense of the situation.

Gibson opened the envelope he held in his hand and pulled out a photograph. "On the night Eddie disappeared I'd just put a new film in my camera and being a keen photographer I was hoping to get a picture of that tree over there by the caravan as darkness fell so it'd be in silhouette form beneath the new moon, providing the clouds had cleared. It's rather a beautiful shape, don't you think?" Hetty and Jackie glanced at the tree in question and nodded their heads, "Anyway," Gibson continued, "rather than leave it too late I came out to see where might be the best place to stand and found if I stood on the wall you're sitting on, Jackie, then I'd be in the perfect spot. While holding up the camera to view the scene, I accidently pressed the shutter but thought nothing of it and went back indoors hoping to come out again later. As it was the cloud didn't shift and the moon remained hidden and so I didn't take any pictures until the following night." He paused for breath, "Anyway, I've been busy this last week or so but finally got round to developing the pictures yesterday and this is what I found. I'm not into digital, you see. Call me a Luddite if you like. Anyway, this is the picture I took by accident."

The black and white photograph was of the pub's field beneath the dull grey sky and at the back near to Eddie's caravan, two figures were just visible emerging from the gap in the hedge that led onto the cliff path. It was not possible to see any features of the two figures but one was side face on and wore his or her hair in a ponytail.

"That has to be Gemma," gasped Jackie, "I recognise her top."

Hetty nodded. "Just what I was going to say. She was wearing it the other day."

"Are these the girls you were talking about then?" Gibson asked, "The ones that took the harmonica?"

"Yes," sighed Jackie, "They've been staying with us and I've got to know them quite well."

"Well, I've never clapped eyes on them myself and I never even saw them when I accidentally took the picture, but because I knew it'd been taken on the night Eddie disappeared, I thought it might be of some interest."

"Good gracious me," Hetty was almost speechless.

Gibson returned the photograph to its envelope. "So now you see why I think we should phone the police."

"We certainly do. In fact I'll do it," Jackie reached in the pocket of her jeans, "Damn, my phone's at home. I came out in such a hurry I didn't even think of picking it up."

"I should have mine somewhere," Hetty placed her handbag on the wall and shuffled through the contents."

"Do you always take a cumbersome bag with you when dog walking?" Gibson was amused.

"Normally, no, but I don't have any pockets in this outfit and Lottie insists I take my phone when walking Albert alone in case I get hurt or whatever. Ah, here it is," Hetty took out her phone and unlocked it, "Rather than ring 999 I'm going to call Dave because he's familiar with all this." She scrolled through her contacts and found Dave's recently added number.

"Dave?" queried Gibson.

"He's a police officer and Hetty's next door neighbour." Jackie spoke in hushed tones as Hetty's call was answered.

"All done. Dave's on duty and he'll be here directly," Hetty returned her phone to her bag, "Now we just have to keep watch and make sure the girls don't leave before the police get here."

Albert, sensing the walk was temporarily curtailed, made himself comfortable on a paving slab warmed by the sun. As he closed his eyes, the door of the pub opened and then closed.

"Jackie," the tone of the female voice sounded confused, "I didn't expect to see you again so soon."

Surprised to have heard her name called, Jackie quickly turned around and saw Lucy standing in the doorway of the pub taking the van keys from her bag. Behind her was Gemma.

"Oh hi, Lucy," Jackie put her hand holding the mouth organ behind her back and tried to hide her embarrassment, "Yeah, I thought I'd come out for a walk seeing as it's a nice day and so forth and then I got chatting to Hetty and Gibson."

Gemma frowned. "A walk. In your slippers?"

Jackie looked at her feet. "Oh yeah, silly me. I hadn't even noticed."

Gibson clumsily fumbled with the envelope and backed towards his car hoping to pass it unseen through the partly open window. Hetty, to draw attention from Jackie's embarrassment and Gibson's manoeuvre, stepped forward. "Did you have a nice lunch, girls?"

Gemma scowled. "How did you know we've had lunch?"

"Oh, um, Jackie just said. I asked if um you'd gone home yet and she said yes but you were calling in the pub for lunch before you left the village."

"I see, and yes thank you we did have a nice lunch. Scampi, chips and peas to be exact and now we must be on our way." Lucy's hand shook as she unlocked the doors of her van.

"Did you have a dessert?" Hetty knew the question was banal but she was playing for time.

"No, we didn't and before you ask, our drinks were cranberry juice," snapped Gemma.

"Oh, very nice. I do like cranberry juice especially if it's ice-cold."

Lucy opened the driver's door and threw her shoulder bag onto the back of the van. "Anyway, thanks again for your hospitality, Jackie. We really do appreciate it."

"I hope you've not left anything behind," blurted Hetty, desperate to delay them further.

Gemma frowned. "What do you mean?"

"You might have left something behind. You know, something might have fallen down the back of a chest of drawers or got kicked under a bed. These things happen, you know. Tess who is the housekeeper for Sea View Cottage says things get left all the time and she has to forward them on to their owners."

Gemma shrugged her shoulders. "I don't know what you're getting at because we have everything with us that we came with. Haven't we, Lucy?"

Lucy nodded and frowned at the same time.

Jackie, annoyed by Gemma's attitude held out the box containing the harmonica, "Really? Are you sure?"

"What's that?" Lucy stepped forward to see.

"Don't ask me," snapped Gemma, "Never seen it before."

"Well, it was under your bed, Gemma, and it doesn't belong to Norman or me. I'll open it and then we'll see if its contents jog your memory."

"A mouthorgan," said Lucy, "No, it's not ours. Neither of us are at all musical. Are we Gem? Although you're quite good at singing."

"I know it doesn't belong to either of you," said Jackie, "because it has the name Eddie engraved on it."

"Eddie. Is it Eddie's?" Lucy turned to Gemma, "Did you take it from his caravan, Gem?"

"Maybe. After all he won't be playing it again, will he?" Realising what she'd said Gemma tried to backtrack, "That is, I mean, poor Eddie. He's not here anymore, is he?"

At the same time as the confrontation outside the Crown and Anchor, Matilda Haddock was driving towards the village with her son Lewis having collected him from hospital. The fish and chip shop she had left in the capable hands not only of her husband, Garfield, but Dolly and Eve, who with time on their hands, had insisted on helping the Haddocks out for the lunchtime period. As they approached the Crown and Anchor, Lewis shouted to his mother to stop the car. When she drew to a halt he leapt out and pointed his finger accusingly at Gemma. "That's her, Mum. That's the psycho who hit me over the head. I remember her face now as clear as day."

"Well, I never," said Hetty, "You're a right little no-good, aren't you, Gemma?"

Gemma's eyes flashed across the faces watching. "I...I..."

"You hit him over the head? When and why?" Lucy was clearly mystified.

All stopped to listen as from the far side of the village drifted the sound of approaching sirens. With a look of relief on her face, Hetty stepped back and glanced along the main street. "Oh dear, looks like someone's in trouble."

Gemma's eyes flashed. Lucy stood rigid.

"Probably an ambulance," mumbled Gemma, her face white.

Gibson shook his head. "No, it's the police. Ambulances have a different ring."

174

Within seconds, two vehicles pulled up outside the pub with lights flashing; one a standard patrol car, the other unmarked. Two officers stepped from each.

Lucy, her face white, fell to her knees and sobbed. Gemma's jaw dropped, she swore and then seizing the chance to escape attempted to run, but Hetty feeling a rush of adrenaline, raised her hefty handbag and with a mighty swing knocked Gemma to the ground.

# Chapter Twenty-Two

After the police had read Lucy and Gemma their rights, the girls, restrained in handcuffs were driven away in separate cars; Gemma screaming and shouting, Lucy pale and in shock. Before questions were asked, Matilda helped Lewis, confused and unsteady, back into her car and took him straight home. While Jackie, in floods of tears and visibly shaken, was helped inside the Crown and Anchor by James who, along with several of the pub's clientele, had gone outside to see what the noise and commotion was about. Noting her pale face, James asked Hetty in also. Hetty thanked him but said she really ought to be going home. Seeing she was upset and on the verge of tears, Gibson insisted on walking her back to Primrose Cottage, and after telling James he'd be back in due course to book into his room, they crossed the road into Long Lane. At the top of the hill as they turned into Blackberry Way, Hetty asked Gibson in for coffee so that he could help her relay the news to her sister. Inside they found Kitty was there too and before the kettle had boiled, Debbie's car pulled up in the driveway. Lottie opened the door to their friend before she had a chance to knock.

"Lots of excitement in the village today," she gabbled, "I don't know what but I just saw Marlene and she told me that as she came out of the fish and chip shop earlier two police cars went whizzing through the village, lights flashing, sirens blaring, and stopped outside the pub. She didn't have time to go and see what it was all about because the fish and chips would have been cold by the time she got home and Gary was waiting for his lunch because he was due to start work at two. I've just driven by but they're not there now, so goodness knows what that was all about."

"Come in, Debbie and get your breath back. Then you can hear what Hetty has to say. She's not been back long herself but appears to have first-hand knowledge." Lottie closed the door and while Debbie went into the sitting room she returned to the kitchen to make coffee for everyone.

"Oh, hello, Gibson. I didn't realise you were back in the village." Knowing Hetty's thoughts regarding the singer, Debbie was clearly surprised to see him at Primrose Cottage.

"Only just got here," he chuckled, "In fact my luggage is still in my car and I've not yet checked into the pub. The last hour or two have been, well, rather eventful and that's putting it mildly."

"Sit down, Debbie, then when we all have coffee, Gibson and I will tell you the latest." Hetty patted the seat beside herself on the sofa.

Once everyone had a mug of coffee, Hetty, still shaken, told how she was out walking Albert and as she drew level with the Crown and Anchor, Gibson drove into car park. Shortly after Jackie arrived, flushed and out of breath. Gibson then told of the photograph he'd taken and Hetty continued with Jackie's discovery of the mouth organ and the arrival of Matilda Haddock with her son, Lewis. Incidents that impelled them to call the police.

"So are you telling us that those girls were in some way involved in Eddie's death?" Debbie was struggling to take it all in.

"Not just involved," said Hetty, "it looks very much like they were the cause of it."

"What? No. But why? How?"

Hetty drew in a deep breath. "As soon as the police arrived and addressed the girls, Lucy went to pieces. She looked awful and muttered, 'It wasn't meant to be like that. Honestly.' Gemma told her to shut up but she wouldn't and as we stood there utterly astounded in the car park, some of it came tumbling out." Hetty paused and took a sip of coffee, "Honestly, it was awful and I've never heard such language as the girls screamed and hissed at each other while the police tried to restrain them and more and more people poured out of the pub. Anyway, from what we gleaned it appears the girls weren't fans of Eddie at all. Quite the opposite in fact. Gemma hated him and said we'd hate him too if we knew what he was like. She said something about him having abandoned her when she lost her job but we don't know what she meant."

"Lost her job! But I thought they were both students," Kitty, scratched her head in confusion.

Hetty sighed. "I agree, that's certainly what they told everyone."

"Perhaps only Lucy is then. I mean, she must be a student of some sort to be able to design a garden like the one she did for Jackie and Norman," reflected Debbie.

"And if Gemma isn't at uni that would account for the sheepish look when we asked her which course she was taking," said Lottie, "Media studies was probably the first thing that came into her head."

"Something like that," spluttered Hetty. "I can't believe her reaction didn't set alarm bells ringing. But then we had no reason to suspect she was not telling the truth."

"So what happened, Het?" Kitty eagerly asked. "Why come down here to see Eddie if they didn't like him?"

"Would you believe, to blackmail him? At least that was the impression I got. It appears it was all Gemma's doing but again I don't know why." Hetty took another sip of coffee and then addressed Gibson, "Do correct me, please if I get any of it wrong, won't you? It's just my head's spinning after all that screaming and I can't think straight."

"Of course, of course." Gibson brushed cake crumbs from his mouth with a large white handkerchief, "but so far you're spot on."

"Thank you," Hetty then continued, "Well, as I've already said, it appears Gemma wanted to blackmail Eddie but no reason was given and it was difficult to make out just what they were saying because both girls were trying to talk at once. Lucy was trying to demonstrate she was innocent of any wrong doing and Gemma was shouting at her to shut up. The poor police, they had the devil's own job to restrain them both and at the same time try and make sense of what they were saying. But from what I can make of it they must have gone to Eddie's caravan and somehow ended up on the cliff path. Maybe a scuffle broke out and Eddie ended up going over the cliff edge, we just don't know. It must have been something like that though because Gemma kept shouting 'it was an accident'." Hetty paused for breath.

"Goodness me," said Debbie. "So what do you think happened?"

"We don't know," said Gibson, "The girls didn't get the chance to say anything else because by then the police had bundled Gemma into the back seat of one of the cars. However, Lucy managed to shout, 'It wasn't an accident, you pushed him, Gem.' Furious with her, Gemma tried to get out of the car but the police held her back and slammed the car door shut."

"I feel sick," muttered Debbie, "and to think we took that awful Gemma a cake, flowers and chocolates. What mugs we are."

"Well actually they were for Lucy," reasoned Hetty.

"Well, she's no better," snapped Debbie. "They both fed us a pack of lies."

"So when did Lucy hurt her ankle," Lottie asked, "I mean, that injury was genuine enough."

"We assume when they ran across the field to get away as quickly as possible," said Hetty.

"So sad," tutted Lottie, "Despite what you say, Debbie, I feel a bit sorry for Lucy but angry at the same time. I mean, the silly girl should never have gone along with blackmailing."

"She certainly shouldn't. I'm really angry with them both and can't believe we were so gullible. I feel quite ashamed."

Hetty tried to reassure her friend, "The police must have believed them too, Debbie. After all as far as we know they never checked the girls out."

"True, I suppose." Debbie took in several deep breaths to calm her racing heart beats.

Hetty finished her coffee and placed the empty mug on the floor by her feet. "I hope Jackie's alright. Poor soul was really upset and when I think of everything she and Norman did for those girls, well, it makes my blood boil."

Lottie patted her sister's hand. "But at least they'll get their just desserts, Het. Although we'll probably never know whether or not Eddie falling was an accident or if Gemma did push him, but at least the charge will be manslaughter and not murder, as it's obvious murder was never Gemma's intention. As for the blackmailing, well, I suppose we'll never know what that was about."

"Probably not," said Kitty, "but it must have been something quite drastic if she thought it was big enough to threaten Eddie with?"

"It must, but I suppose it's no concern of ours anyway," said Hetty.

"And whatever it was it can't hurt Eddie now." Lottie collected the empty coffee mugs and placed them on the tray.

"Thank goodness we didn't go to the police with the wine gum story." Debbie tried to suppress a smile.

"I think if we had the police might have smelt a rat," said Kitty, "I mean, in retrospect it was pretty daft, wasn't it? On the other hand they'd probably have locked us up for wasting police time."

"And no doubt that and the clumpy walk were drummed up on the spur of the moment to send us on a wild goose chase," Lottie shook her head, "You've got to hand it to the girls, when it comes to spinning a yarn they're both pretty good."

Gibson, having finished his coffee and cake, stood up saying he really ought to get back to the Crown and Anchor to check in. He thanked the ladies for their hospitality and after being assured that Hetty was recovered from shock, left the house and walked down Long Lane mulling over in his mind the bizarre events since his arrival. Shortly after he left, Eve called in on her way home from helping out in the fish and chip shop. "Dolly and I are not going to be charged," she blurted as Hetty opened the door, "The lads have taken full responsibility for the cannabis plants and Dennis has admitted that we would never have broken the law had he not bullied us into it."

"Come in, come in," Hetty closed the door after Eve crossed the threshold. "Does that mean you'll be opening up the pasty shop again now?"

"Yes, hopefully sometime next week. We need to earn some money to pay the mortgage and other bills which are mounting up." She sighed, "I'm not sure whether anyone will come in though, with Jude and Dennis labelled as murderers. If only we could clear them of that."

Hetty, quickly deciding not to say anything until Eve was seated, led her into the sitting room. Eve attempted to smile at the ladies. "I'm sorry, I didn't realise you had a houseful."

181

"No problem. Sit down, Eve," Hetty pointed to the chair Gibson had vacated, "The reason we're all here is because there's been a bit of excitement in the village this morning. You'll never believe it, but the girls staying with Norman and Jackie have been arrested in connection with Eddie's murder."

Eve's jaw dropped. "How? I mean, did they do it then? And if they did, why?"

"Well, it looks like it, in a roundabout sort of way as for why, well, that's a bit of a mystery."

"In which case Jude and Dennis are innocent, just as they said they were." Eve's eyes filled with tears.

"It certainly looks that way," said Kitty.

"I can't take it all in. I've gone all goose-pimply," Eve took a tissue from her pocket and wiped her eyes, "So do you know what happened?"

"We know bits, but to be honest we have more questions than answers."

Lottie picked up the tray of empty mugs. "While you tell Eve what we know I'll go and put the kettle on. Eve looks like she could do with a cup of something. Anyone else for a refill?"

Hetty, Debbie and Kitty all nodded their heads.

Five minutes later, Lottie returned to the room with a full tray just as Hetty concluded her reiteration of the morning's event by telling of watching the police cars drive away.

"What intrigues us," said Debbie, eying the slices of treacle tart on Lottie's tray, "is what Gemma had over Eddie. I mean, it must have been quite something if she hoped to blackmail him because of it."

Eve smiled. "I think I might know and if I'm right it's nothing earth shattering, in fact it's really quite trivial so I'm probably wrong and it was something else entirely."

Debbie's eyebrows shot up. "You have our undivided attention, Eve."

"Well, as I say it probably wasn't this at all, but it's what Eddie told us when he came to the shop for the job interview. Not that you can really call it an interview. It was a friendly, informal chat and that's why he told us what a scamp he'd been when young," Eve thanked Lottie for the mug of coffee and took a sip.

"So are you going to tell us or keep us guessing?" Debbie was on the edge of her chair.

"I'll tell you as long as you promise not to broadcast it all around the village."

"As if we would," said Hetty.

Lottie cast her sister a withering look.

"Good, it's just that Eddie said he didn't mind his friends knowing and most knew anyway but he didn't want to damage the squeaky clean image of the other band members because even though they'd gone their separate ways, they're still friends. At least they were until poor Eddie died."

"We're intrigued," confessed Hetty, "and we promise not to tell anyone except Jackie and Norman. I think it's only fair they know after having the girls under their roof for a while."

"Yes, of course, I understand that and as I said it's nothing earth shattering anyway and probably not even the reason for the blackmail. It was just a bit of naughtiness when they were young. They being Eddie and his then best mate Brad. They were thirteen at the time and lived on an estate where the kids used to hang around in a play area. One day during the school summer holiday a mate of theirs was selling fags for fifty pence each. At that point neither Eddie nor Brad had tried smoking and they thought they'd like to give it a go. The trouble was having both spent their pocket money they were penniless. Now it just so happened that an elderly couple who had a beautiful garden were away on holiday, in Cornwall would you believe, so the boys thought they'd pick a few of their flowers and sell them to get some money. While Eddie picked flowers, Brad ran home to get some elastic bands, a piece of paper and some felt tipped pens to make a price sign. They made three bunches, sold them on the corner for a pound a bunch and then bought some fags. The next day they did the same again but on the third day they got caught. A neighbour who was looking after and feeding the elderly couple's cat, had noticed the flower stocks were depleting and so kept a look out. When she saw them picking flowers she called the police. The boys said they thought it wouldn't matter because the flowers would probably have been dead by the time the elderly couple arrived home. But they were still questioned at the police station with their mothers present. Thankfully the couple didn't want any action taken against the boys even though their parents did and for that reason the parents insisted the boys work in the couple's garden for an hour a day for the rest of the school holiday, sweeping the paths, weeding and tidying up. It all worked out well because they became friends with the elderly couple and Eddie kept in touch long after he left school."

Lottie smiled as she recalled finding cigarettes hidden in a pair of Bill's socks when he was thirteen. "And did the boys take up smoking at that stage?"

Eve shook her head. "No way. Eddie told us after they got caught just the sight of a fag made him blush with embarrassment."

Debbie chuckled. "That's a charming story but I really can't believe it would be enough for Gemma to have blackmailed Eddie with and certainly not something he'd have lost his life over."

"I agree," said Kitty, "the problem now is, if we want to find out the real reason, how do we go about it? I mean, as far as I can see there's no-one to ask."

For once, Hetty, still shaken by events earlier in the day, dropped her usual over-keen stance and said, "I think it best we forget it and let sleeping dogs lie."

# Chapter Twenty-Three

Later in the day, following the arrest of Gemma and Lucy, Jude and Dennis were released from police custody. The charge of murder had been dropped and having pleaded guilty to cultivating cannabis with intent to sell it to dealers, they were released pending further investigation. Their solicitor, however, hoped that since it was a first offence and they had to date received no payment, they might get off with a light sentence or even a caution.

Dolly and Eve, who had driven them back to Fuchsia Cottage, were delighted to have them home, but despite the initial euphoria, Dolly sensed that all was not well and finally Dennis admitted he had fallen for someone else and that he wanted to leave and move in with her at her home in Penzance. Needless to say Dolly was upset and when asked, Dennis confessed to having first met Caroline when they had cleaned her windows back in the summer during the spell when they'd all lived in the caravan while the builders had worked on the pasty shop. He admitted to leaving his number with her and two days later she called him and asked if he'd like to meet up for a drink. He did and it blossomed from there.

After all four had discussed the whys and wherefores, it was agreed that Dennis must go and that the other three would endeavour to raise the money to pay back his input into the pasty shop premises. He left the following morning having agreed with Jude that they continue with the window cleaning business for the time being. The work van was to be kept in Pentrillick and Jude would then pick up Dennis at the end of Wisteria Avenue each morning at eight-thirty. Dennis claimed this was for practical reasons, but having located the property of his new love on-line, the girls knew it would be because a trade van would be an inappropriate vehicle to have parked on a regular basis anywhere in an up-market area such as Wisteria Avenue.

Matilda, glad to have her son out of hospital and home with her and Garfield at Pentrillick insisted he stay to rest until he was back to his old self. "It might take me a while to recover," he'd teased, as his mother had showed him to his room, "my flat in Leeds is tiny. One bedroom, a small galley kitchen and a lounge not much bigger than the shared bathroom."

"Well you're welcome to stay as long as you want, love. I'm just happy to have you here. We've a lot of catching up to do."

"Is it alright with Garfield?"

"Of course. He was only saying last night it'd be nice to have a chap to go to the pub with."

"That's brilliant because I admit I'm very impressed with your set-up here. The flat's gorgeous and being above the fish and chip shop you don't have far to go to work. As for the view from the back windows, well, as soon as this dressing on my head wound's gone, I'll be taking a dip in the sea even if it is September. Meanwhile, I suppose I ought to ring my boss at the garage and tell him what's happened. I've already overstretched my week's holiday."

"I think you'll find he already knows because the police went to see him when they found out who you were. Still be nice if you got in touch though as he's probably wondering how you're doing."

In the evening after they had closed the shop, Matilda and Garfield took Lewis to the Crown and Anchor to meet the locals, knowing many would be eager to make his acquaintance as well as discuss the latest development in the Eddie Madigan case. At first he was hesitant, conscious of the dressing on his head, but Garfield came up with a solution and loaned him a cap to wear.

As they passed opposite the church, Matilda pointed to the spot where he had been found. Seeing the bench at the bus stop triggered a sudden flash of memory. Lewis stopped walking and suggested they cross the road so that he might try and relive the night he was attacked.

He sat down on the bench and closed his eyes. "I remember pushing my bag under the bench then sitting down here while I figured out how best to surprise you. Then out of the corner of my eye I saw someone approaching. It was that young woman, Gemma and she was carrying a bag of rubbish. She pushed it in the bin over there. I said hello, just to be friendly like but she didn't answer; she just stared and my presence seemed to make her nervous. I saw her go over to the church wall and take a stone off the top. I wondered why and then everything went black."

Matilda sat down beside him and squeezed his hand. "She must have thought you were a local and panicked thinking you might tell someone she'd come from the village hall."

"But I didn't know she'd come from the village hall. I don't even know where it is."

"No, but she didn't know that, did she?"

"I suppose not."

Matilda stood up. "It's just a few yards along here, you'll see it in a minute. Come on. Best not to get maudlin. What's done is done and hopefully she'll get her comeuppance."

As Jackie left the Crown and Anchor after her lunchtime shift she noticed several empty glasses on one of the picnic tables in the pub's field. Being conscientious, she went to collect them to return indoors but as she neared the table she heard someone crying. She looked around; there was no-one in the field and the sobbing appeared to be coming from over towards the cliff path. Thinking someone might be hurt or in trouble, she left the glasses and went to investigate.

Sitting on the grass along the edge of a path, a young woman sat hugging her knees; a sea breeze tousled her long blonde hair and tears flowed from her puffed up eyes. Jackie, torn between not wanting to interfere but at the same time wanting to help, chose the humane option and asked if she was alright.

The young woman turned her head. "I had to come and see for myself," her voice was little more than a whisper. "Is this where he fell?"

Jackie felt a lump in her throat. "You mean Eddie?"

"Yes, Eddie. Is this where he fell?"

Jackie sat down beside the young woman. "The exact spot isn't known but it would have been somewhere along here."

"It's all my fault, you know. I should have been with him but, no, because of my stupidity we drifted apart and now I've lost him forever," Her voice shook with emotion, "I've lost all I held dear."

"Willow. Are you Willow?"

She nodded. "Yes."

Jackie wanted to say something but was unable to find the right words. It was Willow who broke the silence, "How do you know who I am?"

"What? Oh, umm …someone saw you mentioned on social media as Eddie's ex-girlfriend and remembered your name. They thought you might be in the village, you see. Then you deactivated your account and people said you'd disappeared. Something like that. I can't remember exactly."

"Someone thought I was in the village. Why would they think that?"

"Because they saw a young female on the pub's field a day or two before Eddie died. Of course it wasn't you; it would have been either Lucy or Gemma." Jackie felt her cheeks burn with embarrassment knowing she and Norman had housed Eddie's killers.

Willow frowned. "You know Lucy and Gemma?"

"Well, yes, sort of."

"Just what do you know about them?"

"That they've been arrested and charged with Eddie's manslaughter. That Gemma wanted to blackmail him and it all went wrong. That Lucy hurt her ankle and so couldn't drive home. That everyone took pity on them, myself included."

"I see, and do you know Gemma's reason for wanting to blackmail him?"

Jackie shook her head. "Not really. It's been suggested it was over some silly juvenile flower selling ploy, but I can't believe that's right if several people knew about it anyway."

Willow half smiled. "No, it wasn't that and as you say, most of us already knew. In fact he was often teased about it and was frequently sent flowers as a joke."

"Oh. So do you know of another reason then?"

"I do and just to put the record straight, when I disappeared it was to stay with my grandparents in Scotland. I was devastated by Eddie leaving me and just needed to get away. And then he died. I came back home two days ago when I learned of the arrests."

"I can understand that. You wanting to get away."

"Good. Anyway, to explain Gemma's reason for blackmail we need to go back to our schooldays. My

189

parents moved from Scotland to Yorkshire when I was fourteen and when I started at the local comprehensive I was put in the same class as Gemma. Eddie was a year above us and Lucy was a year below. Eddie and Gemma were already a 'unit' and their relationship continued for several years after they left school. They still might have been together but then one day someone saw Gemma in a chemists stuffing make-up inside her clothing. They reported it to shop staff. She was arrested for shoplifting and consequently lost her job as a supermarket cashier. Eddie, shocked by her behaviour ended the relationship because by then he and some mates had started Rhubarb Chutney and they didn't want her name to tarnish their squeaky clean image. Gemma was furious at being dumped, but that turned out to be the least of her problems because with a police record she found it hard to get a job and so turned to petty crime. That was a few years ago but it's common knowledge amongst our set that since then Gemma has run up serious debt problems, mainly due to overspending on credit cards and she's been known to gamble on-line too."

Willow stopped talking and gazed out to sea as if in a trance.

Jackie spoke gently. "I don't understand though. I mean, what was her reason for blackmailing Eddie?"

"Sorry, I'd forgotten that was your original question." She took in a deep breath, "During the time Gemma and Eddie were together, Gemma had an accident. Nothing serious. She fell off her bike and ended up with a black eye and a lot of bruises. No-one was with her at the time and there were no witnesses. Recently she's been dropping hints to Lucy that the bike story was a cover-up for the fact Eddie used to knock her around. When Gemma heard Eddie was coming to Cornwall she persuaded Lucy to bring her down here so she could get him alone and blackmail him by threatening to tell all on social media that he'd ill-treated her. Apparently, she wanted two thousand pounds up front and further monthly payments of five hundred pounds in cash for the foreseeable future. For some reason she thought Eddie was loaded. Silly girl. They barely made a living. Anyway, after finding out where he was staying they watched his movements and then one night went into his caravan to confront him. He laughed and told her to get lost. In a rage she grabbed his phone and said she'd write it as a confession on his Facebook page. He tried to get the phone off her but she ran away out here to the cliff path. Eddie chased her and Lucy ran after them both. A scuffle broke out and in a rage Gemma gave him one almighty push over the edge of the cliff. They saw him fall and bounce from rock to rock until they heard a splash as he fell into the sea. They watched but he didn't come up again and so, convinced he was dead, they returned to the caravan where Gemma wiped his phone clean of fingerprints along with all other surfaces they had touched. Lucy was in a state of shock. She wanted to tell the police. She pleaded with Gemma saying they could tell them it was an accident and that he'd slipped. But Gemma said no, good riddance to bad rubbish. As they left the caravan, Lucy's vision was obscured by tears and she fell down the caravan's steps and badly hurt her ankle. She couldn't put her weight on it and so Gemma helped her over to some shrubs where they hid while they decided what to do. Shortly after, a chap carrying a guitar arrived on the scene. They knew he wouldn't hang around if Eddie wasn't there but had to stay put until he had gone. After a while he eventually left and Gemma helped Lucy back to her van. They then went into hiding knowing they couldn't leave because Lucy was unable to drive and Gemma had never learned. So as not to worry people back home, they said they were in Newquay and had tested positive for Covid and so wouldn't be home until they'd done ten days in isolation. By then they hoped Lucy's ankle would have improved and she'd be able to get them back home."

Deeply shocked, Jackie was almost lost for words. "But...but I don't understand. Why on earth did Lucy go along with it?"

"Because Gemma said if she didn't she'd tell people that she was involved with some of the petty crimes too. Lucy knew if she did then there was no way she could defend herself. It'd just be one word against the other. She's very gullible is Lucy and was devastated when while in hiding, Gemma told her that she'd made the whole Eddie knocking her around story up just to get her to go along with it."

"So how do you know all this?"

"Because while Gemma was out one day nicking stuff from the village shop, Lucy sent me a very long email explaining where they really were and what had happened. That's another reason why I stayed so long in Scotland. I was torn between loyalty and doing the right thing."

"Loyalty?" Jackie was confused.

"Lucy. Lucy Mackenzie, was my little sister."

"Was?"

Willow bowed her head to hide her tears. "Lucy died at eight o'clock this morning. We received a call yesterday afternoon to say she'd been taken into hospital and so Mum, Dad and me drove straight down. Lucy had a rare heart condition, you see, and we knew she'd never make old bones. She didn't want anyone to know though. Didn't want the sympathy. Didn't want the fuss, and so we did as she asked and told no-one outside the family. The shock of all this must have been too much for her and her heart gave out."

"And did you get to see her before she...?" Jackie couldn't complete the question.

"Yes, yes, we did."

Jackie placed her arms around Willow's shoulders and hugged her tightly. "I'm so very, very sorry."

# Chapter Twenty-Four

Having just been informed of Lucy's death, Gemma stared at the ceiling of her prison cell and reflected on the folly of her ways, for she knew without doubt that her wayward lifestyle was partly to blame for the loss of her one true friend. Guilt caused her cheeks to redden and her eyes burned with unshed tears; she felt ashamed for having whined on about her own self-inflicted misfortune while Lucy, dear Lucy had listened intently but said nothing of her own life threatening illness. For the first time in her young life, Gemma felt very humble and full of remorse. Fully aware it was not possible to change the past, Gemma resolved to take the moral option and admit that on impulse she had pushed Eddie Madigan to his death and that Lucy had in no way been involved with that final reckless act. Relieved for having made the right decision, she steeled herself for her appearance in court the following morning where she would to plead guilty to the charge of manslaughter and hoped that by doing so, Lucy would be absolved of any involvement posthumously.

After her encounter with Willow, Jackie offered to drive the young woman to Penzance so that she could catch a train back to Truro where her parents had booked into a hotel. Willow, who had arrived in the village by bus, thanked her and on their parting the two young women vowed to keep in touch. When Jackie returned to Pentrillick she drove straight up to Primrose Cottage, for

Norman was working and she needed to tell someone who had known the girls, of Lucy's passing. Hetty and Lottie were both home and Jackie wasn't surprised to find Debbie and Kitty there also. The ladies were all saddened to hear Jackie's news and when Kitty returned home to Meadowsweet, she rang Vicar Sam to inform him of the latest developments. Consequently in church the following Sunday, the congregation were asked to remember in their prayers, not only Lucy Mackenzie and Eddie Madigan, but their young friend who having strayed from the path of righteousness had seen the error of her ways and was full of remorse.

Following the arrest of Gemma and the death of Lucy, Gibson Bailey stayed in the village for a few more days and during that time he became better acquainted with the ladies in Primrose Cottage and their two loyal friends. For Hetty, overcome with guilt for ever suggesting he might be involved in Eddie's demise, wanted to make sure he enjoyed his brief stay. They invited him to join them walking Albert, and took him to visit Pentrillick House. One evening they met up for a meal at Primrose Cottage and on his last night they met for drinks and a meal at the Crown and Anchor where he promised on his return home to forward a CD, made in 2019 of a concert recorded live in Birmingham on which he was one of the performers and sang Lottie's late husband Hugh's all-time favourite *aria*, Nessun Dorma.

One afternoon, feeling subdued, Dee walked down to the village and onto the beach where he threw pebbles onto the ebbing waves. Eddie's death had affected him badly. Not only was it a wicked waste of life and talent but his demise had quashed Dee's ambition to be a musician or indeed anything else. Life felt meaningless.

Sitting at the far end of the beach contemplating his future, retired police officer Paul Fox, watched the lone figure ambling across the sand and shingle. He had heard from his replacement, DI David Bray that his partner's son, Dee Osborne had taken Eddie's death badly and that he blamed himself even though he had no reason to do so. Overwhelmed with a sudden urge to help the lone figure, Paul slipped from the rocks and made his way across the beach.

"Hello," Paul called as Dee, sensing someone approaching, turned around.

"Oh, hi."

"Mind if I join you?"

Dee shrugged his shoulder. "If you want."

Paul walked alongside him. "Having a bad day?"

"Every day's a bad day."

"Every day? I find that hard to believe."

"But it's true."

"So what makes you feel so dejected?"

"Everything, but mainly Eddie. I thought knowing him would help me get into music and stuff. Now not only have I lost him as a sort of friend but I'm back to square one with nothing to get out of bed for."

"Don't let things get you down. Winston Churchill once said, *a pessimist sees difficulty in every opportunity, where as an optimist sees opportunity in every difficulty.* That's well worth remembering."

"Yeah, it's alright for you to say stuff like that. I mean, you've had a successful career as a copper and so you've achieved something."

"But you're still young and have years ahead of you. There's no reason why you can't make something of your life and achieve something too."

"There is when you've got no qualifications. Having said that, I don't need any qualifications to be a musician and play in a band."

Paul laughed. "Maybe not, but you need to be able to play at least one instrument. Anyway, why do you want to be a musician?"

Dee stopped walking. "To be famous, I suppose. Have a nice house, flashy car and be a household name. A bit like the Hamiltons."

Paul sighed. "Fame's not all it's cracked up to be, you know. It comes at a price."

"In what way?"

"In all sorts of ways. Your life's not your own. You don't know who your true friends are and it's a back-stabbing business."

"But surely the money makes up for that." Dee pushed his hands into the pocket of his jeans.

"To a point, yes, but money's not everything."

"It is when you don't have any."

Paul smothered a smile. "Yeah, I suppose so but I daresay many of the rich and famous at some time in their lives were broke as well." He picked up a pretty shell and held it up to the light, "Have you made any friends here yet?"

"Not really, but then I never go anywhere."

"Are you any good at pool?" Paul slipped the shell into his pocket.

Dee shrugged his shoulders. "No idea. Never played."

"Well why don't you go along to the pub and have a go? The new season's just started and I hear the team would love to have a few new members."

"Can't go to the pub. Got no money."

"Don't be such a defeatist. Get yourself a job."

"Where? I don't drive so it'd have to be in the village. Unless I took the bus, I suppose."

"How about the pasty shop? It's opening up again soon so they might need another pair of hands."

"Yeah, but I don't think it'll be open for long. Mum and Dave were talking last night and apparently Mum saw Eve yesterday and she said they are going to have to sell the place because they can't afford to keep it. They've got to buy out the bloke who left to shack up with his new girlfriend, you see, and with the possibility of prison sentences for the blokes for growing weed, it's not looking good. Mum said they'll keep it going until they get a buyer and then go back to wherever they were living before."

"Selling," Paul stopped dead in his tracks, "Bear with me, Dee. I've just had a brilliant idea."

Paul ran from the beach and out into the main street where he hurried along the pavement to the pasty shop. As expected it was still closed but he knocked on the door hoping one or both the ladies would be preparing for opening up again. To his delight, Eve answered.

"I hear you're planning to sell this place and if it's true I have a proposition to make to you and yours."

Eve, taken aback but keen to hear what he had to say, asked him in, where he found Dolly cleaning and polishing the serving counter. To their surprise he asked about the building work needed to make the upper rooms habitable. Eve assured him the building was structurally sound because they had to have a survey to get the mortgage. It was just a case of installing heating, a bathroom or two, replacing some of the cracked lathe and plaster walls and ceilings and rotting woodwork, especially on the stairs.

"Have you had it valued yet?" Paul asked.

"No, but if we can get back what we paid plus the cost of the building work we had done to the shop and kitchen areas then we'll be happy with that."

"Then please allow me to buy it. I've sold my place so there's nothing to hold things up and if you agree I'll have the upstairs rooms renovated for my own occupation and the shop area will be yours for a peppercorn rent for as long as you want. How does that sound?"

Dolly flopped down in a chair. "It sounds wonderful and if that were the case we'd easily be able to afford the rent for Fuchsia cottage."

"And it means we can stay," Eve gave Paul a hug, "but don't you want to see the rooms upstairs first? You might find it worse than you imagine."

"I think I know what to expect but yes, it sounds a good idea."

The upstairs rooms had been cleared of their illicit plants but a faint smell of cannabis still hung in the air. Paul walked from room to room including the huge attic space and then looked from a front window and down onto the street. Above the rooftops of the building on the opposite side of the road the sea sparkled in the late September sunshine.

"I love it and I'll happily pay your price but I have one proviso. That being you offer young Dee Osborne a job so that it might improve his self-esteem."


After lunch the following day, Hetty and Lottie decided to take Albert for a nice, long walk to chew over information received regarding Gemma's arrest, Lucy's death, the rescue of the pasty shop, and at the same time to clear their heads. Earlier in the day, Jude Sharpe had called at Primrose Cottage with a large potted plant for Hetty. He told her how sorry he was for the way Dennis had spoken to Bill and herself and hoped she'd accept the plant as a peace offering. To his delight, Hetty had chuckled, and said 'well at least it's not a cannabis plant'. After that he'd joined them for coffee during which he confessed that in a funny sort of way he was glad they'd been found out. He, like Eve and Dolly, had never been comfortable with the arrangement and he was glad the plants had never had a chance to grow any bigger. And even if they had, he felt sure some suspecting person visiting the shop would surely have identified the strong smell that would have emanated from the plants once they had matured.

The route the sisters chose for their walk was through the village and out towards Little Trenwyn and the lane that led to Pentrillick House but as they passed the charity shop they were drawn to a notice pinned in the window asking for volunteers. Fearing that Daisy and Maisie might be about to retire, they went into the shop to find out. To their relief Maisie told them they weren't retiring but did want to cut down their hours. They had both enjoyed the two occasions when the shop had been closed during lockdowns and thought they'd like to do other things while they were still fit and able. The sisters left the shop wracking their brains trying to think who might be able to help out for a couple of days a week.

"I don't suppose," Lottie slowed her pace, "I don't suppose you'd consider doing it, would you, Het. With me, of course. I mean, it could be quite interesting."

A broad smile crept across Hetty's face and she gave her sister a quick hug. "I was thinking the same thing because right now I feel something worthwhile to occupy our time is just what we need."

# Chapter Twenty-Five

September slipped away quietly and October crept in with a warm and sunny day. Inside the Crown and Anchor and other locations in Pentrillick, chatting villagers commented on the evenings drawing in and the mornings getting darker and while some lamented the passing of summer, others relished evenings by an open fire.

As leaves on the trees began to turn and seed heads formed on summer bedding, Michaelmas daisies and Japanese anemones bloomed in abundance throughout the village, while along the lanes, brambles laden with ripened blackberries, shared the hedgerows with ivy, woodbine, wild fuchsias, bindweed and gorse.

The Hamiltons returned home on October the second. The repair work to the theatre was nearing completion and the production company were eager to gather everyone back together ready to get the show up and running again. From the bench outside the church, Marlene watched as the family drove away from Sea View Cottage. In her heart she was sorry to see them go but in her head she knew it was for the best. It was time to stop day dreaming like a giddy teenager and get back to reality and prepare for the village drama group's next production, a meeting for which was due to take place the following week.

Like Sea View, other holiday cottages in Pentrillick, occupied throughout the summer months, saw the last of the season's guests leave the village one by one, and on the beach, occasional walkers, anglers and beachcombers trod across the sand once crowded with sunbathers, picnickers and swimmers. Meanwhile, in the shops, glittery cards, brightly coloured decorations, mince pies, puddings and all Christmas fare reminded one and all that the festive season was not too far distant.

On Monday October the fourth, the pasty shop reopened with its new member of staff, Dee Osborne, smartly dressed, hair tied back, and understandably nervous. When Eve had called in at Hillside and offered him a job he thought she was joking. But when he realised she was serious he recalled Paul Fox's advice and to his mother's delight jumped at the chance. Meanwhile, there had been another surprise in store for him, for Paul, was an accomplished pianist and guitarist, who until he joined the police force in the nineteen eighties, thought, as did Dee, that his future might lie in popular music. After consulting Margot and getting her blessing, Paul offered to teach Dee all he knew about guitar playing and if it appealed, the chance to learn the piano too. Dee was overwhelmed and for the first time since he'd arrived in Cornwall felt the future held promise.

While customers came and went in the pasty shop below, in the upstairs rooms Paul stood talking with local tradesman Basil, who had been recommended to him by Hetty and Lottie, his current next door neighbours whom he was getting to like more every day. For Paul, having set the purchase of the pasty shop property into action, had moved, on Dave and Margot's advice, from his accommodation in Penzance to Tuzzy-Muzzy, a Bed & Breakfast business and the first house in Blackberry Way next door to Primrose Cottage. This would enable him to be on the spot to keep an eye on the renovation once the sale of the former antiques shop was completed. Basil, the builder in question, who had converted the loft into living space at Primrose Cottage, was happy to take on the work but wouldn't be able to start before the end of November due to other commitments. This suited Paul fine for he thought it unlikely the sale would be completed much before then anyway.

After Basil left, Paul sat on one of the window seats and looked towards the sea. With a chuckle he recalled the previous morning when while chatting to Hetty and Lottie about builders, Hetty had asked if he had been serious when he suggested a joint birthday party. He admitted at the time he had said it in jest but the more he thought about it the more it appealed and so it was agreed that, restrictions and so forth permitting, a party would take place in February at the Crown and Anchor to celebrate their combined birthdays. Something to look forward to during the dark days of winter.

Feeling content, Paul watched a ship far away on the horizon and thought back over the past. He had enjoyed his years in the police force even though some cases had kept him awake at night. He thought of the girl arrested for the part she had played in Eddie's death and the subsequent death of her friend and of Eddie himself. Such a waste of three young lives.


On the back doorstep of their home at Cobblestone Close, Norman and Jackie sat quietly side by side watching two doves splashing around in an old granite birdbath they had rescued from a reclaims yard the previous day and placed in the very spot Lucy had suggested for either a sundial or a birdbath. Following the arrest of the girls, Jackie's first thoughts were to destroy the plans even though she knew to do so would be foolhardy. But Lucy's untimely death and her encounter with Willow had changed everything and instead she and Norman had agreed the garden must go ahead in Lucy's memory. Consequently, a delivery of paving slabs, wood, bricks and a galvanised arch stood at the far end of the garden and between them Norman and Jackie planned to do the structural work over the winter months ready for planting up with Lucy's choice of shrubs, trees and flowers in the spring.

Inside Pentrillick's charity shop, Maisie and Daisy having put forward the names of Hetty and Lottie to the small organisation that ran the chain of three shops for animal welfare in Cornwall, welcomed the sisters to their first of two shifts where they would be shown the ropes. At the end of the second, Maisie and Daisy were confident the sisters were competent enough to be left on their own. And so the following day, Hetty and Lottie manned the shop unaided. However, just in case there should be any problems, Maisie and Daisy left their contact details and said they would call in just before closing time to supervise the cashing up.

After they had opened up and made sure everything was in order, Hetty picked up the remaining string of three coloured glass fishermen's baubles. "These are so pretty. There must be a way we can utilise them in next year's Pentrillick in Bloom competition. Perhaps for the new themed garden category."

"I was thinking along the same lines. How do you feel about having a fishing theme? We could borrow some old nets and drape them over the bare side of the garage wall. Then put sand, pebbles and a few rocks over the soil and incorporate the balls amongst them with a few shells and perhaps even a bit of seaweed as well."

"Oh yes, and maybe we could borrow an old crab pot or two and part-bury some old flip-flops, odd socks, a broken body board and add a few empty beer cans and cigarette butts for good measure."

Lottie laughed. "Are you being facetious, Miss Tonkins?"

"Sorry, yes, and your idea sounds good, but as it's a gardening competition we'll need to have some plants as well."

"No problem there," said Lottie, with enthusiasm, "We'll buy some seeds and grow sea holly and dig up the thrift from our rockery."

"Yes, and we'll try and get hold of sea asters too, and golden samphire and sea campion," Hetty laid down the balls and reached for her handbag beneath the counter. "I'm going to pay for these now and put them aside, before someone else comes in and nabs them." As she took her debit card from her purse, the shop doorbell rang and Debbie bounced in.

"Have you come to see how we're getting on?" chuckled Lottie, as Hetty rang the sale up in the till.

"Or do you have some gossipy news to tell us?" Hetty having completed the sale returned her bank card to her purse and pushed her handbag beneath the counter.

"Well, both, I suppose but I can see you're quite at home here." Debbie sat down on a piano stool, "as for the news, it's about Matilda's son. I bet you didn't know he's going to stay down here."

"Is he? Well I never," said Lottie, "but that'll be nice for Matilda because she said she's not seen much of him these past few years."

Hetty nodded, "So how has this come about, Debbie and how do you know?"

"From Gideon because after last night's choir practice, a couple of the chaps said they were going for a pint and so Gideon went with them. Lewis was in the pub with his step-dad, Garfield. Dee was there too along with Eve, Jude and Dolly who are trying to get him out and about more. There weren't many people there so all were sitting down by the fire. One of the things they talked about was music and Dee said he hoped one day to find like-minded people and start a band. When Lewis heard that he said 'well if you need a drummer, I'm your man.' Gideon then realised that Lewis was intending to stay in the village and so asked a few questions. It seems he liked Leeds well enough but coming down here made him realise he liked Cornwall more. It's all done and dusted anyway because he's already spoken to his boss at the garage where he worked and was told there was no need for him to work a week's notice. Garfield's driving him up there today to collect his belongings from the flat."

"So what will he do down here?" asked Lottie, "Work in the shop?"

"No, as luck would have it he's going to work at Vince Royale's garage. "Vince is a regular at the fish and chips shop and when Matilda told him her son was a mechanic and he'd be looking for work, Vince offered him a job on the spot."

"Lovely," said Hetty, "it's nice to have a bit of good news. I'll put the kettle on to celebrate."

With mugs of tea in hand, Debbie remained sitting on the piano stool and Hetty stood by the counter. Lottie sitting on a pile of books waved her hand towards her sister. "Maisie was telling me that just for fun they use that clear glass fisherman's ball near your elbow, Het, as a crystal ball and take it in turns to make daft prophecies."

"Did she? I didn't hear her say that but what a good idea," Hetty put down her mug of tea, grabbed a floral curtain from the shelf, draped it over her head and waved her hands over the top of the upturned ball, "Bagsy my turn today."

Lottie stood up and moved towards the counter. "So what do you see, Mystic Het?"

"I see a book and on its cover is a beach party."

Debbie laughed. "Ow, what's it called?"

Hetty smothered a smile. "It's called, *High Jinks at High Tide*. It's a romantic comedy written by the one and only, Shelley Sinclair."

Lottie frowned. "Shelley Sinclair! Never heard of her."

"You've never heard of her. My dear, Lottie she's quite famous."

"You're pulling my leg."

"Of course I am. The name just popped into my head and the book title inspiration came from the tide table pinned on the notice board over there." Hetty nodded towards the cork board by the door as she dragged the curtain from her head, folded it neatly and returned it to its other half, "Anyway, I don't know about you two but I think us working here will be very useful when it comes to solving Pentrillick's next crime. What with a crystal ball to assist us, and shops being good places for gossip, solving a crime should be a cinch."

Lottie looked alarmed. "You think there'll be one then?"

"Oh yes, Lottie. Just you wait and see. And on top of that, next year we have, providing of course there are no Covid restrictions, Zac and Emma's wedding in September and our joint birthday party with Paul in February. There's also the Pentrillick in Bloom competition with its new theme category. Queen Elizabeth's Platinum Jubilee celebrations in the summer and the drama group's next production. After all the doom and gloom of the past eighteen months, I have a feeling that 2022 will be the best year ever."

Debbie leapt to her feet and raised her arm. "Yes," she cried, "Bring it on."

Printed in Great Britain
by Amazon

79355372R00122